The Lost Children

The Lost Children

Donald Willerton

Terra Nova Books
SANTA FE, NEW MEXICO

Library of Congress Control Number 2016959827

Distributed by SCB Distributors, (800) 729-6423

Terra Nova Books

Published by Terra Nova Books, Santa Fe, New Mexico.
www.TerraNovaBooks.com

ISBN 978-1-938288-77-7

For My Mother

CHAPTER

Ouray, Colorado
August 19, 1891

I t is my secret. It has been my secret from the beginning. *My secret and not hers. I wish I had never told her!*

Jessie Jacobson raised up on her knees against the side of the wagon as it bumped and jarred its way over the rutted dirt road, then sat with her back against the boards, then switched to hanging her arm over the side. She looked forward, straining to see ahead, wanting to be there.

Is Maggie already there? Will she go to the cabin without me? Will she . . . ?

Jessie couldn't sit still, both anxious to be done with it and terrified to see it through.

Has she already blabbed it to everyone? What will she do when she sees that I left the key at home? Will she be angry?

She's ruining everything!

Jessie's father used a flick of the reins to make the mules pull harder, the wagon jerking as the team heaved it over the last rise. The road flattened, and Jessie reminded herself that it was only minutes to the picnic area. It would soon be over.

Jessie's dad guided the wagon to the hitching fence that had been built the previous year. Several dust-covered wagons and carriages had already pulled up and tied, depositing a crowd of townspeople—families, the town council, visiting dignitaries, miners, and railroad men. Bales of hay had been spread among the animals, both as feed and to keep them from snipping at each other.

Among the trees, bright red and white tablecloths were spread over boards set on more than two dozen sawhorses. A parade of food baskets was emptying onto the tables, which were soon crowded with homemade pies, fried chicken, hams and turkeys, deer and elk stews, beans, breads, mashed potatoes, and huge crocks of brown gravy.

"You get your fingers out of the chicken, young man," Sally Jacobson scolded her son as their baskets were lifted from the wagon bed.

"Can I go now, Momma?" Jessie asked.

"No, you may not. There is work to be done getting all the food laid out and then I expect we will hear a few speeches from the mayor and others. You're old enough to hear what they have to say. You and your brother grab those pies and be careful with them— they're still juicy."

"Ugh!" little Matthew wailed. "We don't have to wait for everybody else to eat, do we? I'm hungry now!"

"I'll have no more of that," his mother warned. "Speeches first, then we eat. You can go play if you want, but you watch for when we start eating or there won't be any food left when you get back."

Maggie Thayer trotted over to Jessie. Jessie stiffened and held her head a little higher than normal.

"Come *on!* You know you want to," she said, and then turned toward Jessie's mother. "Can Jessie go now, Mrs. Jacobson? Can she?"

"Jessica has to be patient and so do you, Margaret. We've got to get this food to the table."

Maggie didn't like it when people used her full name, Margaret. It sounded formal and proper, and that was definitely what she did not want to be. She wanted to be like her father.

Maggie Thayer was Jessie Jacobson's best friend, or had been until recently. The girls' mothers often wondered why the friendship always seemed hot or cold, but decided it was just the nature of the girls themselves: Jessica was responsible like her mother, with more than her measure of discipline for her twelve years. On the other hand, Maggie, a year younger, was red-haired and boisterous, loud, sometimes careless, and constantly full of energy.

"Like trying to hitch a wild mustang to a carriage," her mother had said on more than one occasion.

"You children come here before you set off," Jessie's father said. "You be careful if you go into the forest, you hear? Jessie, you take care of Matthew and don't go off leaving him."

"Yes, Poppa," Jessie replied. She knew she had to take care of Matthew   he knew where they were going and she had already bribed him not to tell. Part of that bribe was that he got to go along.

"I was expecting Jessie to listen to the speakers," Sally said to her husband. "She's old enough that she ought to be paying attention to the workings of the town."

"Listen to the speakers? *We* don't even want to listen to the speakers; they'll talk for hours and never say anything.

Besides, Jessie does more chores than the rest of the girls her age. She ought to go off and play. She's earned it."

Her mother was not convinced but gave her permission just the same.

"And don't you children go stirrin' up any ghosts," a voice said over Mr. Jacobson's shoulder. "You don't want ol' Crazy Bill to rise up and start ticklin' your toes!"

"Brewster Thayer, don't you go scaring these children, you hear me?" Sally said as she gave him a stern look with raised eyebrows.

"Cross my heart, Sally. I'm just lookin' out for the safety of these here children," Brewster replied, smiling until she walked back toward the wagons. He turned back to the young ones gathering around him. "You kids know about ol' Crazy Bill, don't you?"

Several more children ran up and joined the group, knowing that Mr. Thayer, Maggie's father, was about to tell one of his stories, something he was famous about town for doing. It wasn't unusual to find him at the Ouray Mining and Mercantile Bank, feet propped up on his desk, leaning back in his big chair, wistfully recalling a story about someone or other having some kind of adventure while they were out on the wild plains, or up in the mysterious mountains, or maybe it was out on the great oceans of the world. He wasn't a man to be bothered with the facts. He believed no story was worth telling if you didn't help it along.

"It was ten or fifteen years ago, I disremember exactly, that they found his body in the cabin, the very cabin that's right up in those trees. Well, yes, I do remember that it was about this time of year, when the moon—well, gracious me—was almost full, just like it will be tonight!"

A little girl squealed.

"Ol' Crazy Bill lived up there all alone, hardly ever coming to town except every month or so to buy food and tobacco. Well, it hadn't been any more time than that, so nobody would have known anything was wrong if it hadn't been for his mule. That mule showed up one day, trotted right through town, and went directly to the feed trough over at the livery. The blacksmith knew the mule belonged to Bill, so he walked over and told the sheriff about it.

"Ol' Bill had been a prospector 'round these parts for a number of years and the rumor was that he had struck a gold pocket somewheres in these mountains. But he kept the location secret.

"Well, the sheriff didn't mind riding up and checking on ol' Bill, thinking that maybe he'd come across him while he was working his claim. But instead of finding the man working, he found him inside his cabin, sitting at the table, dead as a doornail, and under some mighty peculiar circumstances. Must have been dead for a week or more, but that ain't what was peculiar.

"Ol' Bill's body was like he had froze to death, but it weren't cold at all. His body was hard as a stone statue, and it was all crooked and twisted so bad they had trouble getting him out the cabin door. His arms and legs were bent in every direction, so much so that the undertaker had to cut them off to get the body inside the casket!"

"Brewster, I declare!" Sally called with a warning look.

Brewster continued in a lower voice, "I knew some of those who helped carry him back down the mountain. They was saying that the body was bad, all right, but it was his face that gave them a fright. His eyes were bulgin' out of their sockets, his ears and nose bloody, his lips pulled back so all his teeth was grinnin' a smile from the devil himself! And it was the devil who killed him too. The doctor said as much.

"Scared to death! That was the doc's judgment. It wasn't written down as the official cause of death, you understand, but that's what the doc said all the same—I heard him myself. It took courage for the man to admit it. It must have been ghosts or demons or the dogs of hell. He had been scared to death, like Ol' Crazy Bill had seen the very face of Beelzebub!

"But that wasn't the end of it, no sirree. I've heard stories that his soul was left behind in the cabin, a ghost now, just waitin' for some little child to wander by!"

A little boy began to cry and ran for his mother. Some of the children squealed in glee at Brewster's story while others weren't sure whether he was telling the truth or making it all up.

Jessie's face had turned pale while Maggie tried to stifle her laughter with her hand.

"Thank you very much, Mr. Thayer," Sally Jacobson said sternly, shaking a wooden spoon in Brewster's direction. "You children go play, but you stay away from that cabin, you hear me? And stay away from cliff edges, and the bottom of the falls, and any other place you can think of that I would tell you to stay away from, you understand?"

There was a furious nodding of heads as the children scattered in a half-dozen directions toward the various places to play in the deep canyon of Thunder Falls.

High above the picnic area, a mountain stream poured over a cliff, cascading sheets of water several hundred feet to the canyon floor, the noise of the water hitting the bottom and echoing off the steep canyon walls with a roar like continuous claps of thunder. Outside the town limits a couple of miles, up a steep road that took the town folk above the narrow confines of their houses and streets, the waterfall—so big and so close—was the pride of the town, a place to relax and enjoy the beauty of the mountainous backcountry of Colorado.

Thunder Falls and its canyon provided a place for the community to gather and socialize and the children to play. The children's favorites included the swings that had been built near the tables, the pile of big rocks at the base of the falls where they dared each other to run through the spray from the splashing water, and the dense forest that naturally led to games of hide and seek.

The men played horseshoes, held knife-throwing contests, hosted shooting matches and, on special occasions, set up ropes for a boxing ring and had a few locals toughs go at it. Ladies preferred to sit around the tables chatting.

For the hardy and adventurous, several trails led in and around the canyon. One trail led up the side of the mountain into the peaks above.

Once the tables were set, Sally Jacobson became more sympathetic toward her husband's opinion about speeches. After the dignitaries had gathered at the front of the crowd, it was almost an hour before the exhausted audience finally fell upon the feast laid before them.

Afterward there were games, battles at the horseshoe pits, sack races, and an instance or two of settling the horses after a few of the boys were careless with firecrackers.

Only when the cleanup had begun and baskets were being carried back to the wagons did Sally worry about her children. She couldn't remember seeing them during the meal, nor at the games.

The sun had crossed over at mid-afternoon and the shadow of the mountain now covered the canyon floor, giving the air a late-summer chill. Jessie and Matthew's jackets were still bunched on the wagon seat.

"Oh, don't worry," Mr. Jacobson said. "Matthew wasn't about to miss his helping of chicken, so I'm sure he and Jessie made it to one of the tables, ate their fill at someone else's expense, and went back to play. They don't get much chance to go their own way with their chores and all, so let them have their freedom for a while." His wife reluctantly agreed, but didn't like it.

A half hour later, after some of the wagons had pulled out for town, Sally decided that enough was enough. Her husband and Brewster Thayer began casually walking around the falls looking for the kids, up some of the trails, and along the road back to town.

An hour after that, the search became more serious, with all the remaining men fanning into the forest and up the sides of the canyon, looking along the streams, checking the boulders at the base of Thunder Falls, checking the bottoms of the cliffs. Some of those already in town returned to help.

Families were interviewed and the rest of the children counted. There were three children not spoken for.

Three children had gone out to play and hadn't come back.

A rain that night kept the hounds from being used until morning. But the handlers told the families it was no use, that the rain would have washed away any scent. They were right. The dogs only roamed in circles as they bayed.

Some of the men climbed the trail out of the canyon and into the basins below the peaks, checking old mine shafts and abandoned buildings. Others went through the forest along the road to town while others explored every gully for a mile around, peering over cliffs and into crevices for any signs.

People searched for days. Nothing was found.

In the end, there was only heartbreak and sorrow and rivers of tears.

Three precious children.

Lost.

CHAPTER

The Present

"Quit daydreaming and hold it tighter."

Mogi Franklin turned his attention back to the butcher paper he was casually holding with his fingertips. Jennifer was smoothing out the rest of it, adjusting the edges, folding it carefully around the curved top of the gravestone, and occasionally stepping back to make sure it looked straight.

He lifted the paper slightly and pulled, smoothed it across the upper edge, then returned to looking at the distant town nestled between the still-snow-topped mountains. Huge thunderheads were building around the peaks, billowing and white on top, dark and threatening on the bottom. Like clockwork during the summer, Ouray, Colorado, would soon have its daily shower. The rain would stay in the area around the peaks and would not come into the valley north of town, which Mogi thought was good since he and Jennifer hadn't brought umbrellas.

He and his sister had taken a local's advice and were visiting the town's cemetery, some five or six miles down the highway from their cousin's apartment. When their cousin Jimmy had invited them to visit, and offered a free place to stay, they couldn't turn it down.

Jennifer was delighted to come to the cemetery, while Mogi thought it would be boring. It was proving, however, to be the highlight of the day. The cemetery was quiet and peaceful, the trees and grasses were rich with full-bodied smells, and the hundred or so ancient headstones were fascinating and sobering, making him wonder what life had been like so long ago.

"I bet it's already a hundred and ten at home," he said, giving a slight smile as a cool breeze made him shiver. The people in his hometown of Bluff, Utah, would already be heading indoors for the day so they could plop down in any spot that would shade them from the sun's intense noon heat. The barren, parched, slickrock country in the summer was like the inside of a furnace.

Situated above the banks of the San Juan River, less than an hour from the Four Corners Monument, the country around Bluff included hundreds of square miles of bare sandstone, with solitary mesas rising for a thousand feet out of the desert floor and an uncountable number of craggy, twisting canyons. It was stark, beautiful country, but living there was sometimes brutal.

Thinking about the heat at home and how he would usually be either firmly planted in front of his computer and Xbox or working at some part-time job that always seemed to involve being out in the hottest part of the day, he stared down the cool, green valley and found himself completely satisfied with taking Jimmy up on his offer, even though his cousin was a lot older than he was.

Mogi was fourteen and tall for his age, but his muscles had not yet caught up with his bones, so he was gangly and spindly and a little awkward, which is to say, normal for his age. He took after his mom's side of the family in his looks and his shyness, but seemed to be a sum of both families on the brain side: He was typically way smarter than the people around him, quick-minded, mentally disciplined and orderly, and had a natural talent for handling information.

Jennifer was seventeen and definitely took after their father. Shorter than her brother by a half-foot, with thick, brown hair cut short, she was strong, athletic, and physically graceful. She had unusual emotional stability for her age, and loved being around others. Whereas Mogi was the obsessive, analytical, adventurous problem-solver, Jennifer was the cautious people person. He pushed her to do more than she thought she ought to; she pulled him back into what seemed more reasonable.

Both of them had great Franklin smiles.

Satisfied that the paper was finally as close and secure as it could get to the gravestone's surface, Jennifer took a stick of charcoal from a box and made circular motions across the paper. Then she repeated the process, moving the charcoal up, down, and sideways.

Gradually, along with cracks, marks, and chips, the letters and carvings of the headstone came through on the paper:

Harriet Johanssen
b. 1856
d. 1894
Beloved Mother, Honored Wife
The Angels Took Her Too Soon

After moving about the gravestone, leaning over to rub for more detail and stepping back to see her work, Jennifer finally removed the paper, laid it on the grass, and lightly sprayed it with hair spray to keep the charcoal from smearing. Then she wet her hands with glass cleaner and wiped them on a paper towel.

"Why didn't you just take a picture of it?" Mogi asked, clearly not appreciating the effort she had put into the rubbing.

"For your information, dork-boy, I did take a picture of it, but you're missing the point. It's not about recording information. It's the shape of the stone, the carving of the letters, and the cracks, as well as the saying; it's how it feels touching the stuff growing in and around the letters. A gravestone has more than just words.

"The last action on earth that honored Harriet Johanssen was this gravestone being set. It was a statement that she lived, a symbol that she existed and somebody knew it, and that she was loved.

"I'm going to frame this and put it on my wall at home. When I see it, I'll think of this place and remember that she was somebody's wife, and somebody's mother, and that she mattered to them. That lets her memory live a little bit more."

Mogi wasn't sure he wanted to wake up each day and be reminded that Mrs. Johanssen had died. He wandered away as Jennifer cleaned up, happy to browse through the meandering rows of graves. Several had variously decorated iron fences, long since bent and warped and aged like the stones they guarded. Most of the gravestones still had dates that were readable: 1893, 1912, 1897.

Who were these people? What was it like to live back then?

The cemetery wasn't big, but it had character, a solid feeling that its inhabitants were resting in peace. Grave-

stones, railings, iron gates, and some larger pads of speckled granite ran in irregular rows through the shade of tall
cottonwoods. Gnarled roots rose and fell from the deep
green grass, lightly worn footpaths circled in and around
the stones, and there were splotches of yellows, blues, and
reds from flowers—some real, some plastic—and a scattering of small American flags.

"Hey, Jen, look at this one."

It was a much larger plot than the others, flat, with no
signs of a grave or gravestone, surrounded by an intricate,
once-black, wrought iron fence. It had not one marker
but three—three small granite statues evenly spaced across
the grass.

The statues were angels, kneeling with hands clasped
in prayer, peering downward with wings spread.

As Jennifer approached him, Mogi knelt to read a faded
metal plaque fastened to the iron uprights. The engraved letters were hard to make out through layers of lichen and rust.

"Let me have a sheet of paper and your charcoal," he said.

He creased the paper's edges around the plaque, and
Jennifer helped to hold it in place. Mogi rubbed vigor-
ously, learning quickly that making a good rubbing wasn't
as easy as it looked. He tore up his first attempt and started
again with a lighter touch.

The letters formed words, and the words finally formed
an unusual poem:

> Our hearts are as empty graves,
> Our minds are as lost footsteps,
> Our souls are as wisps in the wind,
> But our love is forever, forever.
> We trust in God that you knew.

There was no date.

Mogi read the words again but couldn't make sense of them. Who was the "you" in the last line? What were the angels for? Why three? Why would someone go to the trouble of making a grave space so long ago and then apparently never use it?

"How strange," Jennifer said.

"Do you think Nancy would know anything about it? She grew up here, didn't she?" Mogi asked.

"Maybe. We can ask her at lunch. I haven't wandered as much as you, so I hate to go, but we're supposed to meet her at 12:30."

Mogi cleaned the charcoal dust from his hands and took a few pictures of the angels and the plaque as Jennifer sprayed the rubbing. Waving the rubbing through the air to dry, he folded the sides over to protect the lettering, undid one of his buttons, and slipped it inside his shirt.

*   *   *

Mogi watched the downpour through the window at the end of the table. Jimmy, a waiter during the summer, had shown him and Jennifer to a table in the back dining room of the Big Corral Steakhouse, a laid back, popular restaurant on the north side of town.

"Good thing we got here when we did," Mogi said. "I believe the heavens openeth up and dumpeth upon the earth."

Jennifer laughed as she ran her eyes over the menu.

"Hi, guys!" Nancy said cheerily as she approached the table and sat down. Mogi smiled. Jimmy had good taste in girlfriends. Not only was she beautiful but she also had a real job working as the editor and writer for Ouray's newspaper, the *San Juan Mountains News-Herald*. She'd made a success of her first job after college, Jimmy said, while he was still shuffling back and forth in the fall and spring finishing up at the college where they'd met.

"It is *so* beautiful here," Jennifer began, leaning over the table to be heard over the noise of the lunch crowd. "We roamed around this morning and ended up at the cemetery where I got a rubbing from a gravestone. Nobody would mind that I did that, would they?"

"Oh, I wouldn't think so," Nancy said. "There're a few people who are anxious to keep the tourists as confined as possible to the major attractions, but most of us are happy to share whatever you find. What we've got is pretty special and it's only by freely wandering around that you get to experience it."

Mogi noticed her face become clouded as she continued.

"Of course, if you're going to wander for free, you might want to do it pretty quick. Looks like there'll be a whole new ballgame here pretty soon."

Jimmy brought the drinks, took their orders, and rushed away to meet a wave of new customers coming through the door.

"What do you mean?" Jennifer asked.

"Does the name 'Millennium Corporation' ring a bell? Have you seen the posters around town?"

Jennifer thought for a moment. "I don't think so."

"Well," Nancy continued, "the Millennium Corporation is an international syndicate of resort towns. They go around the world looking for small resort areas with big tourist potential—skiing, scuba diving, art centers, big music locations, or even historical places like around Washington, D.C.

"When they find them, they offer the existing communities a package deal—sell the town to them and they'll put a billion dollars or so into transforming the area into an internationally recognized high-dollar resort. It can change a backwater town into an Aspen, a Vail, or a Lake Placid.

"This winter, the Millennium Corporation offered to buy Ouray."

Jennifer's head leaned forward as her eyes grew bigger.

"Buy Ouray? What do you mean? Buy the buildings or something?"

"All the buildings, businesses, streets, sewer system, bridges, attractions, garbage trucks, hospital, county museum, even the shovels people use to shovel snow in the winter—everything. The people here now can remain if they choose, but they become 'employees' of the corporation. Even the individual houses are purchased and then leased back to the families living in them.

"In exchange, the corporation upgrades the utilities, rebuilds the roads, installs full-service communications capability, puts a new coat of paint on every house, rebuilds the historical structures, puts in a new water tower, you name it.

"And then, to make their money, the corporation builds a huge, brand-spanking-new ski resort in the mountains west of town, a monstrous network of ski lifts and runs that will cover several square miles of the high country. They'll build a series of gondolas too that start from downtown and go up the canyon into Yankee Boy Basin, where one of the ski areas would be, go over Imogene Pass at a nifty thirteen thousand feet, and down into Telluride, connecting to its already big ski area. Very European.

"Looking at the plans, it might possibly become the largest ski area in the world."

A different waiter appeared with plates of hamburgers and fries. He passed them around, refilled the drinks, and moved on. Ignoring the conversation for a few seconds, Mogi attacked his mound of french fries with a river of ketchup.

Jennifer was at a loss for words.

"Is this a good idea?" she finally asked. "Do people want this?"

"There're a number of people who would be millionaires overnight, and the land values would skyrocket for a hundred miles in every direction. It would probably mean more gross income in a year than the total value of all of the gold and silver ever taken out of these mountains.

"Personally, I think it stinks," Nancy said bluntly. "I've lived here all my life. Lots of people have. That graveyard you were in is full of people who shed blood, sweat, and tears making a life here. It's not just a question of money, money, money. It's supposed to be about hopes and dreams and people and love and family and . . . ."

Finishing his hamburger and idly stealing fries from Jennifer's plate, Mogi listened more closely.

"You sound pretty steamed," Jennifer said.

"Well, yeah, I'd say I'm pretty steamed," Nancy said. "This has been a land of opportunity for a hundred years, and I don't deny that wealth has always been a motive for people to be here. But once people bury their families in a place, it becomes much more than just a place to collect a paycheck. This isn't just *a* town—it's *my* town. The idea that I have to become an 'employee' to live here makes me want to throw up."

"Oh, I have a question," Mogi suddenly remembered, unbuttoning his shirt and taking out the folded paper. "We found something strange at the cemetery. An iron fence was around a gravesite, but there didn't seem to be any grave in it, only three statues of angels. It had this funny poem on the fence."

He shoved his empty plate to the side and carefully positioned the rubbing on the table. Nancy read through it.

She smiled. "I haven't thought about them in years. That's the grave—well, what was supposed to be the graves—of the lost children. It's an old story from 1890-something where three children disappeared from a town picnic. Every third-grader in the Ouray public schools learned the story by heart as a lesson against wandering away from school functions.

"The kids were from prominent families—a girl and a boy who were the children of the general store owner, and a daughter of the town banker. They were about ten or twelve years old, old enough to take care of themselves in the woods.

"Ouray had thrown a big celebration when it officially became a city. One of the activities was a community picnic at the base of Thunder Falls, which is a big waterfall up a canyon east of here and a popular place for social gatherings. The picnic was sponsored by the town council and the railroad. A lot of families took their wagons and made an afternoon of eating and playing games.

"Of course, once everyone got to the waterfall, there was a horde of children that scattered in every direction. At the end of the day, when everyone was ready to go, all were accounted for except those three children. They were nowhere to be found.

"The townspeople spent days and nights looking for them. Every man in town helped, and the railroad even gave their workers a day off to help with the search. Nothing was ever discovered. Absolutely no clues, no clothing, no tracks, nothing. They had vanished into thin air.

"The town was pretty much devastated. Kidnapping wasn't a big thing back then, and no ransom note ever showed up anyway. In place of any real information, people made up stories, especially those who blamed anything out of the ordinary on ghosts.

"After a while, the town went back to normal, but the families of the children were devastated. A year after it happened, they hired someone to create a statue of the three children. The sculptor created a clay model that was then bronzed in Denver. It's a magnificent piece of work. It was erected at the bottom of the falls, but was moved later to be part of the county museum. I'm pretty sure it's still there.

"A couple years after that, both families decided to leave and that's when they created the burial plot with the three angels. I suppose they wanted to make sure that if the children were ever found, there'd be a place for their bodies. That's also, by the way, why there's no date."

"That's awful!" Jennifer said. "How sad."

"I can tell you, as a tale to make a third-grader think twice about wandering off, it had a great effect. I had nightmares for a week," Nancy continued. "And I never, ever wandered off from any picnics."

"Do you remember the names of the children?" Mogi asked.

"I don't think so," she said. "I'd have to think about it."

He looked again at the words from the plaque: "Our hearts are as empty graves."

He folded the rubbing, put it inside his shirt, and then sat back, wondering.

How could three children just up and disappear?

CHAPTER

Mogi watched with apprehension as the large rock loosened, scooted downward, rolled slightly, and then let itself go, first with a small riffling sound as it slid down the gravel and off the edge, and then with silence as it fell what seemed like a thousand feet.

Seconds later, a sharp hit of rock on rock produced a loud crack that sounded like a rifle shot; the rock had hit the granite surface of the mountainside and shot back into the trees.

Everything returned to silence, except for the screaming of the Jeep's passengers, each of them instinctively rising up and leaning uphill as the Jeep tipped sideways off the road.

High on the side of a mountain, far in the Colorado backcountry, winding up a steep, narrow, four-wheel drive road, Jimmy's Jeep Wrangler had gotten too close to the road's edge, suddenly slid sideways as the mounded gravel along the cliff gave way, and then sank to a stop with the two passenger-side wheels hanging over hundreds of feet of empty space.

As it settled, the front tire had nudged the large rock off the embankment and down the almost perpendicular slope to the valley below.

Mogi stared through the Jeep's door-less doorframe at the air below him and felt a hard twist in his stomach. He froze as he strained to control his fear and his impulse to panic.

Before the Jeep jerked a couple more inches and teetered to a stop, Jimmy spoke in a low voice.

"Okay, do *not* make any sudden movements. Everybody get out on my side. Mogi, you go over me—I'm keeping my foot on the brake. You girls make it over the side. Go, go, go!"

As fluidly as he could, not wanting to make any jerky moves, Mogi raised up, placed his left foot on his seat, and stepped his right foot over Jimmy's lap to the door opening, carefully avoiding Jimmy's arms, which were gripping the steering wheel. Then he took a giant step onto the rocky jeep trail. It was a few seconds before he could take a deep breath.

Jennifer and Nancy had already scrambled over the open side of the Jeep and were backing across the road when Jimmy turned off the motor, eased on the emergency brake, and rolled out his doorway headfirst with his hands to the ground. He was on his feet and backing away in a flash.

The talking exploded all at once.

"Holy-moly, I think I wet myself," Jimmy said. Humor was always his first means of defense against embarrassment. He moved to the front of the Jeep and bent down, looking under the vehicle. "Oh, man, I was lucky with that one. Everybody okay?"

"I will never, ever, in no way will I, under any circumstances, am I ever going to set foot in that Jeep or any Jeep forever and after, and you will never, ever, nooooo way ever get me on some fool rock pile that they call a road, not ever again!" Jennifer said.

Mogi bent down to look underneath the Jeep as Jennifer carefully reached behind the seat and pulled out her day-pack. She put the pack on and stood away from the others.

He saw that the only thing that had kept the Jeep from slipping down the mountain slope was the front and back differentials—those watermelon-sized pieces of machinery on the axle between the wheels—burying themselves in the slight rise of gravel along the side of the road.

"Well, big guy, if real mountain men drive Jeeps, what do real mountain men do now?" Nancy asked.

"Hmm . . . uh . . . well, let's see here. I guess we need to think about this," was the only reply Jimmy could come up with. "I guess it's time to take a break," he said with a silly grin as he reached over the side of the Jeep and carefully opened the cooler in the back.

Nancy moved away from the Jeep to the inside of the trail and found a rock to sit on. She coaxed Jennifer to sit with her as the boys passed around drinks and snacks.

Mogi walked up the trail a few feet and turned around slowly. They must have been at eleven or twelve thousand feet in altitude. There were still snowdrifts in the meadows, as well as snow on the north side of the peaks. It would be July before all the snow melted away, if it did at all.

The high mountain meadows around Ouray were still shaking off winter, soaking up the warm sunlight, and radiantly spilling colors across the vast expanse. Taking his camera out, Mogi took a panorama of flowers of deep blues, brilliant yellows and purples, soft reds, and carpets of tiny white blossoms against the greens of the hardy high-country tundra.

Watching the small display on the back of his camera, he hoped he had captured it all. While he had the camera out, he took a picture of the forlorn Jeep, imagining the story that he and Jennifer would tell their parents about their adventure.

Or maybe not.

It was Jimmy's day off, and he had talked the others into hiking to the top of one of the mountain peaks close to town. Jimmy's choice was Mount Sneffels, a rugged peak standing like a fortress over Yankee Boy Basin, a series of large mountain meadows with lakes and streams. It also gave Jimmy an excuse to show off his driving skills on the backcountry trails.

But at this point in the trip, it was unlikely anyone would be impressed by his driving skills.

A few minutes had passed when two huge four-wheel-drive trucks ground their way up the road behind the stranded vehicle. These were serious mountain machines—one-ton pickups made with flatbeds instead of the usual pickup beds. With the addition of chest-high pipe rails around the outside and bench seats on the decking, the flatbeds were transformed into mobile viewing galleries for about six or eight adventurous tourists.

Jimmy recognized the two drivers. They worked for a backcountry tour company during the summers and were regular customers at the restaurant. After teasing him and joking around, the first truck squeezed by the small Wrangler and hooked a massive chain onto the tow hook of the Jeep's front bumper. The other truck did the same for the rear bumper, cinching the chain tight and creating a sort of anchor.

The first truck gave a loud whine in low gear as it moved toward the inside of the road, dragging the Wrangler's front wheels onto solid roadbed. It then served as the anchor as the second truck pulled on its chain, cutting sharply to the left, dragging the back wheels away from the edge, giving an extra foot just to be sure. The passengers in the big trucks applauded as the drivers climbed out and bowed to the audience.

Mogi and Jimmy unhooked the chains and dumped them back into the equipment boxes on each of the trucks.

"I, uh, promise that I'll watch the road a little bit closer, really," Jimmy said in a humble way. Mogi and Nancy took their seats. But it took several more minutes to convince Jennifer.

The short wheelbase of the Wrangler exaggerated the jostling, jolting, jerking, jouncing, bouncing, bumping, and banging as it continued on its way up the rough jeep trail. Mogi soon forgot the mishap once Jimmy pulled alongside a lake that was as pretty as any calendar picture he had ever seen.

"It's all footwork from here," Jimmy said. Spilling out of the back, Nancy and Jennifer handed out daypacks filled with food, raincoats, and pullovers.

A mile and a half along the basin brought them to a landslide area. Looking upward, the slope curved directly up the side of the mountain and ended along a ridge of ragged rock. A trail had been carved across the face of the slope, zigzagging as it made its way to the ridge.

"Shouldn't we be worried about rockslides?" Jennifer asked.

"Naw," Jimmy replied. "When there's a lot of snow on it, there's avalanche danger. But without snow, it's just a big pile of rocks that's been stable for hundreds of years. If the rocks were going somewhere, they would have done it by now. Once we get past the first few switchbacks, we cut across the slope and hit the ridge to the peak. It's been a trail long enough that it's even got grass growing on it. We'll be fine. We'll go slow."

Going slow was not a problem. Mogi was soon sounding like a steam locomotive, with a huff, a puff, a wheeze, and a gasp, struggling to take in enough air to make up for the lack of oxygen. Bluff was a whole lot lower in elevation and had a whole lot more oxygen in the air. Jennifer struggled as well, but more disciplined breathing made her less entertaining to the others.

Nancy and Jimmy made the upper trail first and moved quickly across the slope. Mogi, trying to suck deep breaths, helped pull Jennifer the last few yards and then welcomed the easier pace across the slope. A few minutes later, crossing a small snowfield, they reached the ridge. Nancy and Jimmy were sitting down, munching on snacks from their packs.

Jimmy pointed ahead of them.

The peak of Mount Sneffels was about two hundred yards away, clear against the blue sky, a jagged, gray-brown point of exposed granite with a narrow apron of green grass. The dark colors were set off by white snowdrifts. Once on top, they would be more than fourteen thousand feet above sea level, one of the highest points in the United States.

Following his protein bar with a gulp of water, Jimmy led the way to the summit. Once there, Mogi balanced his camera on a boulder and set the timer to get a victory picture as the four of them crowded onto the very top rock.

That done, Mogi sat and looked around. There were mountain peaks everywhere, with an uncountable number of granite spires, rocky cliffs, green slopes, snowy crevices, and expansive basins between the peaks. He guessed they were looking a hundred miles in every direction.

Jimmy took out a trail map and laid it between them. He pointed to the map with one hand and to the scenery with his other.

"You see the plains in the distance," Jimmy said. "That's toward Montrose. Gunnison is off to the right. Directly that way is Telluride, and you can see Mount Wilson and Wilson Peak behind it. They're both 'fourteeners.' Durango must be over there, and that way would be Colorado Springs and Denver."

Listening to Jimmy explain, Mogi gazed at the expanse of the basin below, the big lake at the bottom looking like a blue puddle fringed with green carpet.

"Where did you say the ski resort was going to be built?" he asked Nancy.

Nancy pointed to the road on the left.

"We came up right over there, where the canyon broadens out into a valley. Everything west of that point and within the circle of these peaks is referred to as Yankee Boy Basin. We're sitting on the north side of the basin. All of Yankee Boy Basin, plus a smaller basin to the south, plus all the peaks within those two basins, become part of the resort area. The resort village and the condos will be scattered along the floor of the basins. The gondolas will be everywhere, but the major line going to Telluride will cross on the other side of that ridge over there."

"Wow," Mogi said.

"Of course," Nancy continued, "they may have to 're-model' things with a little dynamite. Take out a peak here, blow up a ridge there. With so many mountains, who would miss one or two?"

"What about the mines?" Mogi asked, pointing below.

Southwestern Colorado was littered with hundreds of abandoned mines. Gold mines, silver mines, you–name–it mines. A few major operations had created vast networks of tunnels under the behemoth mountains, but most had been a single shaft that an individual or small group had dug.

All the mines that Mogi could see had been played out, appearing now only as holes in exposed rock faces, or with skeletons of wood buildings clustered together. All had large cones of tailings below the entrances—rock and debris dug from inside the mine, either dragged in sleds or moved in small ore carts and dumped onto the slope below. They represented the remnants of the gold and silver frenzies that defined Colorado in its heyday.

"Mines are too dangerous to make anything commercial, so they'd be either gated closed or have the entrances filled up," Nancy added.

"Wow," Mogi said again.

He was thinking of all the effort involved in digging a mine in the first place. It must have been viciously hard work, digging into pure rock with picks and sledgehammers, working every minute of daylight, putting up with the dust, dirt, heat, cold, and constant fear of cave-in, not to mention worrying about dynamite.

"Some of these mines employed hundreds of miners," Nancy said. "That's how the rich people of Ouray got rich. Any place you look in this country, there are mines—every mountain, every valley, almost every cliff has been dug into by either individuals or mining companies. Some of the mines struck gold or silver or other valuable minerals, but most didn't. The majority of individual mine owners never made a nickel.

"People got by, though. It was everyday life for a lot of people. Businesses supported the miners, other groups came to support the businesses, towns came to support the groups. People liked what they found and built houses, schools, churches, public buildings. It was hard on everybody, especially when the prices of gold and silver went down, but while some of the people pulled up and left, lots of people didn't. They stayed. They stuck it out."

Mogi looked at the valley in the beauty of summer and imagined it in the harshness of the winter. Those people had to be strong. They had to have courage. They had to learn to survive.

They must have been extraordinary people.

CHAPTER

Four hours before, Mogi had been walking in snowdrifts, and now he and Jennifer were relaxing in an ocean of hot water on the north end of Ouray. At least it felt like an ocean. It was the biggest swimming pool he'd ever seen, its water piped in from natural hot springs at the south end of town. He couldn't help but smile as the warm water seeped into his muscles and erased the aches and pains from climbing.

I was meant to live in Colorado, he thought as he slipped beneath the surface.

Nancy had set their schedule for the remainder of the day. After returning from Mount Sneffels, Mogi and Jennifer could experience the town's million-gallon outdoor swimming pool, then meet her to eat gourmet pizza for supper, and then visit her house to see the puppies.

It was all fine with him.

It was six when the Franklins made it to Nancy's house. Though not among the oldest historical buildings in town, her house was still a large, solidly built, nineteenth-century Victorian home on the west side, a hundred feet up a sloping mountainside. An oak stairway in the center of the house led from the spacious living, dining, library, and kitchen areas on the first floor to bedrooms, baths, and sitting rooms on the second floor. A large attic filled the spaces below the steep roof and its gables.

Wallpapered in rich burgundies and blues against the polished, dark oak flooring, every nook and cranny was filled with antiques. Looking east from the large porch wrapped by white wood columns, the view of the town was extraordinary. The lights sparkled like a field of stars as dusk moved into night.

"This is awesome!" Jennifer exclaimed after a tour of the house. "It's just the kind of house I pictured in a town like this. It was nice of your mom and dad to move closer to your grandparents to help them out, but I bet they look forward to getting back to the mountains. What was it like growing up here?"

"Well, to be honest, not as great as you might think," Nancy said as she sat in a wicker chair. "You had to be willing to entertain yourself most of the time. For adults, there were always things to do—jeeping, hiking, camping, backpacking, peak climbing, rock climbing, yada, yada, yada—but kids were often left out of the equation.

"There was no empty land available for building any- thing new, and the town was never willing to tear some- thing down to build a recreation center, or a dance hall, or a new gym, or anything. Every time a building was suggested for replacement, there'd always be somebody who wanted to preserve it as a national treasure.

"That left us without a place to hang out except school and downtown, which the businesses didn't want because we got in the way of the visitors. We had the swimming pool, and the one little park, but that wasn't much. It's one reason my parents bought this house, so we could have a pool table and ping pong in the basement and a place we could invite our friends over."

Jimmy and Mogi were on the grass in front of the deck, letting two golden retriever puppies pounce between them. They were beautiful puppies, not more than three months old.

Jennifer was relaxing in a rocking chair next to Nancy, leaning back and enjoying the view, breathing the clean air, when Nancy's cell phone pinged. She stood and moved into the house to answer it.

"Being the editor of the paper in this town is not easy," Jimmy said after Nancy left. "She's got a really hard job listening to everybody's gripes. There are a *lot* of tourists and they bring in a *lot* of money. But apart from the ice climbers in the winter, most of the tourists only come in the summer. Durango, Telluride, Vail, Aspen—they all have ski areas that keep the economy going through the winter. There's always money flowing. In Ouray, a lot of businesses just shut for the winter and the owners go back to Texas or Florida.

"Well, okay, maybe I shouldn't be too negative," Jimmy added. "We have great Christmas and New Year's celebrations, with fireworks and everything, and those fill the town for a week or two. Then there are some hotels, some shops, and some restaurants that stay open all year, but they mostly support the local population.

"Not having a booming economy all through the year makes it so the town can't find enough money to maintain everything. The streets are expensive to keep up, the cell service needs updating, and improving the sewer system would be a major project for any city, much less a small one. Of course, no one wants to raise taxes, but even if they did, they still couldn't collect enough to cure all the long-term problems.

"The newspaper is one of the businesses that go all year, so it becomes 'information central' for the towns-people. Nancy was already the neutral diplomat between different camps of locals and then—bang!—the billion-aires waltz in and want to take over the town. This Millennium stuff is eating her up."

Nancy came back onto the porch.

"Well, this will make tomorrow an eventful day," she said as she sat down. "I now have a meeting with Mister Big himself, the CEO and president of the Millennium Corporation. He wants a chance to experience some of the local color, so he's going to lower himself to meet with the town riffraff."

Jennifer moved off the porch, scooped up a puppy, and placed it on Nancy's lap.

"So we'll wait till tomorrow for more news," Jennifer said as Nancy was smothered with a wet tongue and a cold nose.

"The older I get," Nancy said, "the happier I am just to have friends, a quiet town, and small surprises. Oh, hey, let me show you something." She put the puppy down on the porch, went into the house, and returned carrying an old camelback trunk. She set it next to the steps.

It was no more than two feet long and a foot or so high and wide. The top was humped in the middle about four inches higher than the sides.

"You might have noticed an old hotel on the south end of Main Street. It's a famous hotel that's been here since 1887. It was a first-class hotel, and at one time, the grand-est in Colorado. Teddy Roosevelt even stayed in it once.

But the ups and downs of the world wars and the Depression kind of torpedoed it, along with the rest of the town. There have been a number of owners through the years, including one lady in the '50s who went all over the countryside buying every stick of antique furniture she could find, trying to make the hotel into an 1890s western palace.

"But we couldn't compete with Durango, and the hotel was too large to make a profit. The last owner finally closed it and walked away, leaving all the furniture and furnishings.

"It was bought this spring by Millennium as an expression of their credibility. To their credit, they're renovating the hotel to its original appearance, rebuilding it from top to bottom to make it modern. It'll look like the grand hotel that it was in 1887, but it will have modern rooms, furnishings, bathrooms, internet, and everything else you would expect from a good four-star hotel.

"Well, right after buying it, they sponsored a day where the locals could go through and buy furniture, fixtures, or rugs for bargain prices. I found this being used as a toy box in a nursery off a bedroom suite."

The trunk was covered on top with dark, tarnished metal stamped with little stars, with wooden trim along the top, bottom, and sides of each face.

"Oh, what a find! This is darling!" Jennifer said. She lifted the lid. The sides and bottom were covered with faded wallpaper that was cracked and water-stained around the edges, but the hinges were in good condition, and the dull black latches were unbroken.

After running their hands over the top, ooohing and aaahing, she and Nancy returned to their chairs discussing how it could be refinished. Mogi and Jimmy continued playing with the dogs on the grass.

It wasn't long before Jimmy moved the trunk to the grass and was putting the puppies inside it, watching them jump out, putting them back in, running after them, putting them back in, and so on.

Mogi watched.

Two puppies go in the trunk and one climbs out. Now there's one puppy inside and one puppy outside. The outside one struggles to get back in while the inside one climbs right out. The outside one can't climb in because he's not tall enough.

Mogi helps him back in, and then puts the other puppy on the outside. Two puppies—both the same size—one inside, one outside. The inside one gets out easily, but the outside one has to be helped in. One gets out. One doesn't get in.

Mogi leaned over the trunk and inspected the inside.

"Look at this," he said to Jimmy. He ran his right hand down the inside of the trunk while running his left hand down the outside of the trunk. His right hand hit the floor of the trunk a good two inches before his left hand hit the grass. Mogi checked the underside of the bottom. It was flat all the way across, connected to each of the four sides.

"This trunk has a false bottom."

Mogi moved it back to the porch. Nancy, Jennifer, and Jimmy gathered around as Mogi did his hand trick again. With puzzled looks, they did the test themselves.

There was no question—the inside bottom of the trunk was significantly higher than the porch deck. Mogi ran his hand around the inside bottom of the trunk.

"The wallpaper is really thick. Do you . . . uh . . . think we could . . . uh . . . cut it?" he asked Nancy.

She looked at him and made a slight smile. "Let me get a knife." She disappeared into the house and returned with a small utility knife.

The others watched as Mogi made slow, repeated cuts along the bottom edge of the inside of the trunk, revealing several layers of wallpaper. With the final cut, he poked his finger around all the edges, looking for some kind of hold to be able to catch the bottom and pull. He tried wedging the knife blade between the floor and side of the trunk. Even when he did get a grip, the layers of wallpaper wouldn't let the edge budge.

Nancy knelt beside Mogi and took the knife.

"I bet you were never one to rip open Christmas presents either," she said. She took hold of the cut edges of the paper between the blade and her thumb, then ripped the wallpaper up the side of the trunk. "I was going to redo the inside anyway, right?"

The paper was old and stiff and didn't tear well, but Nancy eventually scraped enough layers from the edges to expose the seam of the trunk's floor. She pressed the knife into an edge, cut slightly into the wood of the floor, and pulled up. The floor came loose. Slowly, she lifted the false floor enough to wiggle a finger underneath and pulled it out of the trunk.

A musty smell of oldness rose up as four faces crowded in to see.

Slumped into one corner of the true floor were a worn and tattered doll, a small book with a cracked leather cover, a key, and a small, threadbare blanket, the kind used to wrap newborn babies.

Nancy reached for the doll. "Look at this!" she exclaimed, laying the small doll in her open hand, gently supporting it. Mogi reached for the key, and Jennifer picked up the book.

Jimmy whistled. "Man, oh man! Who would have thought? We found somebody's hiding place! Uh, oh," he said quickly and moved to the far parts of the yard to collect the puppies.

Mogi looked at the key in his hand. It was not a skeleton key, like the kind used on doors, nor was it a modern key with a ridge of cut metal. It was about two inches long and built around a shank that was hollow, like a little pipe. Made that way, the key would only fit a lock with a steel pin in the middle of its opening. On the end of the shank, a small, flat piece of metal stuck out at a right angle with the front edge cut in a stepped fashion. To open or close the lock, the key's hollow shank would be put through the lock's opening onto the pin and then turned.

Mogi inspected the false floor. From the underside, he could see that it had been cut from some kind of thin board, maybe the side of a wooden crate. It had been reinforced with thick paper glued against the wood. Small pieces of wood had been glued around the inside of the true floor so that when the false bottom was laid into the trunk, the wood pieces held it up, leaving enough space to hide things.

"Hey, listen to this." Jennifer was back in the rocker, curled up, reading the book she'd removed. "It's a diary, written in pencil. The handwriting is not very good, but listen. The first page has this written on it:

This is my diary and don't read it if you are not me!!!

"Oh, on the inside of the front cover, she wrote her name. I think it must be . . ." Jennifer said slowly, "Jessica Jacobson."

Nancy was startled.

"That's one of the names!" she cried. "Jessie Jacobson! She was one of the lost children!"

CHAPTER

Mogi stood on the asphalt outside Jimmy's apartment, moving his arms from side to side and stretching his back, then bent over to touch the ground. Behind him, Jennifer cushioned the screen door to keep it from banging and joined her brother in the parking lot. It had been about midnight when they returned from Nancy's house, and Jimmy was due to work two shifts that day, the first beginning at eleven.

It was a typical high-mountain valley morning—brilliant sunlight that arrived late on the streets because of the surrounding mountains, and a light blue, cloudless sky. In the shadows, a mist still hung over the grass, and a chill gave a bite to the air. The asphalt was wet, adding an oily odor to the fresh, thick fragrance of the surrounding trees.

"Are you still interested in looking for the lost children?" he asked his sister.

"Looks like a perfect day for it, as long as we can start with coffee," Jennifer answered. "And we should find the waterfall Nancy talked about. I'd like to see it."

With one cup of excellent coffee and another of hot chocolate from a local cafe, the two adventurers walked to the county museum. Mogi was impressed even before going inside. It looked like a gothic mansion—three stories of granite blocks, round tower-like rooms on the corners, lots of large windows with intricate wood trim, and tall doorways with massive oak doors. According to a brochure, it was built as Ouray's first hospital in 1887. Going through several identities since then, its rooms were now used by the historical society for displays, literature, artifacts, and records. The basement had been converted into an authentic interior of an old mine.

"I hope you're not in a hurry," Mogi said. "I'm guessing that I'll be a while."

"Wander to your heart's content, dork-boy. I'm on a mission."

Jennifer wasted no time in talking to the woman at the counter about the lost children. She was obviously happy to be asked and walked Jennifer through a series of ancient newspaper articles in a display.

Reading quickly, Jennifer finished the articles and scanned through a shelf of local history books for sale. Thumbing through the third one, she stopped at a full-page picture of the bronze statue Nancy had described, *The Lost Children*.

As she held it up for better light, her eyes glanced outside to see the same image through the room's side window. She returned the book to the shelf, found the side door, and stepped into a small flower garden. She followed a brick sidewalk to the statue.

Jennifer was captivated by what she saw. The two girls and the boy were life-size, and the attention to detail was remarkable. The faces, the hands, the texture of the clothing—it seemed as if real children had been frozen in bronze.

The inscription at the bottom read:

Margaret Anne Thayer
Jessica Jacobson
Matthew Jacobson
August 19, 1891

The earth took our children
before our hearts were ready,
but our love remains.

Jennifer ran her hand over the faces of each child, finding the bronze cold and damp.

Jessica was the strong one, she thought. You can tell by the way she holds her head and stands up straight. The smaller girl had more wild in her face, and the boy reflected innocence.

Their clothes were plain, the dresses simple with a bit of lace, the suspenders common to little boys who grew too fast, and high-topped shoes for them all. As Jennifer moved her fingers back to Jessica's face, an object caught her eye. Expertly done, a delicate, heart-shaped locket hung around the taller girl's neck.

It was the kind of locket a mother gives her daughter.

Jennifer moved her fingers across it, feeling the detail, admiring the simplicity, imagining the bond between the mother and her daughter and the deep sorrow the girl's mother must have felt.

Mogi joined his sister at the statue, silently watching her move as if she were in a trance.

Jennifer finally turned her head and spoke to him. "They really did vanish. It was a big picnic, and there were lots of people. They ran into the forest to play and never came back. The canyon with the waterfall isn't even that big, so they literally searched every square inch of the canyon, a mile up and all the way back to town. The first night, they even searched by lantern in the rain. The three kids just . . . disappeared." She turned back to the statue and again touched the faces.

"You want to see the waterfall?" Mogi asked. "The lady told me how to get there." He already knew the answer, but he hesitated to interrupt the intensity his sister was feeling about the statue.

Mogi had thumbed through a picture book of Ouray history by the time Jennifer drove the winding road and pulled into the Thunder Falls parking lot, where there were a half-dozen cars. A few groups of people walked along a path that started in the trees. The bottom of the waterfall was hidden around a curve about a quarter-mile up the trail, but Mogi could see the white cascade of water high above as he opened the car door.

"No wonder it's called Thunder Falls," Jennifer yelled as she and Mogi picked their way to its bottom. It was enormous, the sound deafening. The ground shook beneath their feet as the water crashed into a massive pile of boulders and rocks, splashing water into a huge plume of mist and cloud. A person could climb into the cluster of boulders and walk directly into the plummeting water.

Overhead, the waterfall was the last in a series of pour-overs from the cliffs high above, a large stream fed by water from snowmelt and springs in the high-mountain basins above the Ouray valley. Finally rocketing over the edge more than six hundred feet above the valley floor, the water exploded against the rocks with the sound of a fully revved jet plane.

As Mogi took pictures, Jennifer walked back to the car, got the sack full of goodies from the deli-mart, found an empty picnic table, and ate cookies and sipped a bottle of water while she waited.

"You know," Mogi said when he came back and sat across from her. "It doesn't make sense. Look at this place. If you had a hundred people with stakes, you could probably put a stake on every square foot of this area in a couple of days. Where in the world would three children go that they couldn't be found?

"If we ignore the idea of alien body snatchers, it's not possible."

CHAPTER

Nancy's meeting with the CEO of the Millennium Corporation was held at the municipal building's town council chambers. With her were the newspaper's publisher, Tim Shifley, and its only full-time reporter, Robin Dubane. The mayor and other town officials were already in the room, thickly huddled around their guest.

Henry David Williams had been a lawyer, a stockbroker, and a stock analyst before he joined with a small company of other businessmen who put their money together, found the investment capital they needed, and jumped into the entertainment business with both feet, creating musical venues; buying, managing, and selling record labels; developing luxury hotels; buying a TV network; and underwriting several Hollywood films.

In a short time, they had built an incredible amount of wealth, then split off the company's ventures and divided them among the partners. Williams had chosen the resort side of the business, and established the Millennium Corporation to focus on buying, selling, developing, and managing resort properties.

Though she was skeptical about his intentions, Nancy found herself liking him, realizing that he was not what she had imagined. Instead of seeming extravagant and arrogant, he appeared to be open, honest, and humble. Rather than throwing his weight around and intimidating people, he treated his company's offer for Ouray as only one of many choices its residents had, and hoped it was the best one.

He was not shy, however, in pushing for his objective: He wanted to buy Ouray, from the town limit on the south to ten miles beyond the limit on the north. He needed to acquire other properties to implement his plan of connected ski areas, such as the high country basins and their access roads, as well as water rights, but he had already developed the political backing to know that he'd get whatever he wanted.

Henry David Williams left no question about his beliefs or his motives. He felt he offered a good vision of how Ouray could be reformed in the present and positioned for decades in the future. He wanted to build the greatest vacation resort in the world. He'd make plenty of money and the corporation would make plenty of money, but so would the residents of the town. There would be far fewer problems for individuals to solve or pay for. It could still feel like a little town but would operate like a significant center of Colorado's economy.

Nancy couldn't help but feel the pull of his positive attitude. He had already offered the newspaper's staff, including Nancy, a role in his marketing department. They would be involved from the beginning in developing the corporation's vision for the entire area and would help the company preserve its "feel." And, if they chose, they would be welcome to join the Chicago or New York offices.

New York!

Nancy felt dazzled.

"I have family ties to the mines in Pennsylvania," Williams said, "and I know their proud traditions and values. Believe me, I want to preserve Ouray's traditions and values and elevate them into a set of core beliefs for the leadership of the Ouray enterprise. We can work as a team to not only offer the full range of vacation services for every single customer but we can also surround them with a culture that upholds the character and historical patterns of the people of this wonderful area."

Could this guy talk or what?

A tinge of excitement shivered up Nancy's back. What a challenge—and she could be a major player!

Williams was on a tight schedule for meeting a movie producer in Telluride, so he excused himself early from the meeting. To continue in his place, he introduced Montgomery Harrison, the Millennium Corporation's director of planning and design.

Harrison took over the meeting like a general takes command of an army. Short and to the point, he handed out a thick booklet with the details of the proposal and delivered a presentation with a laptop and projector.

Ouray would be owned by the corporation—all of it, down to the water in the swimming pool. The businesses in town would become subsidiaries of the corporation. The hotels would remain intact, but the owners and managers would be replaced with corporation employees. Any business owners not willing to be bought out would be filed against by the "town," which would then condemn the property, and it would be acquired by the corporation.

Harrison indicated that the compensation for the change of ownership would be an offer no one could refuse—more money than they ever imagined.

"What about the newspaper?" Tim Shifley asked suspiciously.

"The newspaper puts out its final edition the day before the contract is signed. After that, the paper will be produced once a week by our marketing department in Chicago. You'll receive the articles electronically and then compose and print the paper locally. Your current personnel will remain in town to handle the printing and distribution and to give the paper a local face. You'll be allowed to fill a half-page with local information, but all other articles will be reviewed and approved by the Chicago office."

Nancy, having been encouraged by the CEO, felt her enthusiasm fall away, and anger began to seep into her voice.

"What you mean is the newspaper would not be a *news*paper at all," she said. "It would be a glossy corporation advertisement from front to back."

Montgomery Harrison leaned over the table toward her, giving her a fake smile that indicated he did not welcome criticism or sarcasm.

"Welcome to the world of big business, kiddo," he said, as if speaking to a child. "The purpose of all publications within the corporation is for building profit share. That's where the money comes from to pay your salary.

"We are working right now on some logos for the town, the ski areas, and the new Valley Village condominiums and townhouses that will be built in the cemetery area after the cemetery is moved. We'll find another place for it. People don't like living next to cemeteries.

"The logos will be included in all our literature and on all uniforms worn by corporation employees. The newspaper will use these logos to advertise the services, attractions, housing, businesses, and the other profit generators. Part of the paper will also be in different languages—Chinese, Japanese, German, French, and Spanish—as the publication will be targeting the overseas audience as well. Your observation is exactly right: It definitely will not be a *news*paper. Any other stupid questions?"

Nancy did not reply.

Montgomery Harrison finished his PowerPoint. The mayor and some of the others were all smiles as they shook hands, patted him on the back, and escorted him out to continue with a tour of the Yankee Boy Basin area.

Nancy had more comments, but she kept her mouth in check. She was raging inside. The name "kiddo" had ticked her off, but by the time he got to describing her question as "stupid," she was thinking about hitting him with a chair. She wondered if Henry David Williams knew how much his "corporate values" talk was being trampled on by his director of planning and design.

She was glad the meeting was over.

CHAPTER

Mogi leaned back in his chair and smiled with satisfaction. The Big Corral was his kind of place. Good food, good music, irresistible aromas, and great steak. No one was in a hurry. The customers were all relaxed and enjoying themselves, and there was little enough noise in the evening that he could be part of a conversation without everyone shouting.

It made for a good end to the day. He was impressed with the statue at the museum, but walking the waterfall area was his high point. They had walked from the entrance to the falls, up into the forest, around the parking lot and picnic area, and up a trail. It gave him a feeling for what it might have been like for lots of adults to be meeting, talking, and enjoying each other's company while their children ran around and played.

It also gave him a feeling for why three children's vanishing didn't make any sense at all. It was driving him crazy.

"The statue of the children is remarkable," Jennifer said to Nancy. "Whoever did it was really good. Did you notice the locket around Jessica's neck?"

"That's really something, isn't it?" Nancy responded. "I used to dream of having my own mother give me something like that. Talk about special! I can see Jessica's mother working really hard with the sculptor to get it just right."

"When Jennifer was about to start crying all over the statue and embarrassing me," Mogi said, "we went up to Thunder Falls. Now, that was really something. We hiked up a trail that led to a basin. Wow. My legs are still hurting."

"Did you find Crazy Bill's cabin?" Nancy asked.

Both Mogi and Jennifer looked at her blankly.

"There's a side trail that splits from the one you hiked. It's obvious if you're looking for it, and if you follow it, there's a ruin of an old miner's cabin. It's a local legend that there's a ghost who hangs around the place, but the real story is almost as fascinating.

"Around 1870 or so, a hermit built a remote cabin on a rock shelf to the west of the waterfall. A few years later, he died this horrible, awful death. There was never any explanation of what he died of, but the descriptions of his corpse were very graphic. After he was buried, people refused to go into the cabin, so it sat empty for years and years. It's been the source of a lot of ghost stories, like apparitions, screams, strange lights, and dead animals found all over the place.

"Sometime in the 1950s, I think, a hunter from Kansas died while using the cabin during a hunting trip. It was ruled a hunting accident, since the guy actually did shoot himself in the head. The rumors were, though, that it was the ghost who made him do it.

"The city tried to renovate the cabin and make some kind of display of early mining history, but getting to it was so difficult that the effort fizzled before much was done. They put a new roof on it in the '70s, put a new door on, and locked it up for a while. The door was the first thing to go, of course. Somebody carried it off or burned it up. The vandalism was so hard to stop that the city finally gave up."

After Jimmy had stopped by to check on drinks and take orders for dessert, Nancy continued.

"It was a big thing in junior high to dare somebody to spend the night inside the cabin. We always heard that someone did, but they probably stayed long enough to sneak outside and spend the night in the woods. It was fun to make up stories about seeing a ghost, but nobody really believed it."

"I remember reading a reference to Crazy Bill in a book I bought at the museum," Mogi said. "It was a pretty spooky story. I suppose it's a given that they looked for the lost children there?"

"I'm sure they did," Nancy replied. "I imagine that the cabin was one of the first places they went."

The conversation moved on from the children and Crazy Bill to the more-immediate problems of running a town so dependent on tourism.

"It's a roller coaster economy," she said.

"Speaking of the economy, you were going to tell us about your meeting with Mister Big," Jennifer said.

"As much as I hate to admit it, I liked Mister Big. The guy who came with him, though, was a total jerk. Him, I could have smacked."

Nancy looked up at the ceiling and struggled with her next sentence.

"I don't know what to think. Henry David Williams, the CEO, came across as a really nice guy who wants to create a world-class resort that would keep the town the way it is, with all its values and small-town atmosphere, while adding the attractions that would bring in lots of wealthy people. Everybody who had anything to do with it would make a ton of money out of the deal, and the town would prosper as never before.

"He talked well, and I believe he's sincere. He also knows the difference that it's made for other places, so I'm sure that he believes 100 percent in what he wants to do.

"On the other hand, if the second guy who did the presentation has anything to do with it, his priority is that the corporation gets exactly what it wants. He'll make sure that everybody knows the company is in charge and they don't dare do anything against it. The bottom line is to make the most money possible for the corporation's investors, so complete obedience to the rules would be the key principle.

"I can live with making a lot of money, and I can even believe that the benefit to the area is worth more than the desires of any individual, but something inside is telling me I'd be making a deal with the devil. The more I think about it, the more I feel like I would be violated.

"Do you know . . . do you know they want to dig up all the graves and move the cemetery, just so the owners of their new condominiums wouldn't have to look at it?"

Mogi almost knocked his glass over. "They shouldn't . . . it wouldn't be right! It would be like sitting on somebody's grave; you just don't do that. You have respect for certain things." He was imagining the three angels being plowed up by a bulldozer.

Jennifer continued to talk with Nancy, and the conversation moved to the management of the newspaper. Mogi stood up and walked around the dining room, looking at the old pictures of Ouray on the walls and reading the descriptions. There was something about the people in those photographs. Old faces. Tough faces. There was a determination, a spirit, something that looked back at him.

It was getting late as he returned to the table. Jimmy sat with them for a few minutes and then excused himself to straighten the chairs and clean the floor.

"Time to call it a night," Jennifer said. "It's been quite a day."

CHAPTER

8

The morning brought a slow, constant rain. Jimmy opted to work the lunch and dinner shifts again so he could be free the following three days. Jennifer and Mogi would spend this day on their own and then Jimmy would join them for sightseeing during their remaining vacation days. One day would be devoted to riding the narrow-gauge railroad from Durango to Silverton.

Jennifer drew an overstuffed chair up to the rain-splattered window, wrapped herself in a blanket, and continued reading Jessica Jacobson's diary.

Having finished his two Ouray history books, Mogi skimmed through the magazines lying around Jimmy's apartment. Jimmy was not a creative reader, he decided, so he turned on the TV, surfed through a few channels, and then turned it off. Mogi read his email, checked the headlines of the news, found nothing interesting on Facebook, and returned his iPad to his suitcase. Wishing he could go for a run but not wanting to get wet, he looked out the window. The rain was lessening, but it still piddled a million circles in the puddles of the parking lot.

"So, what's in the diary?" he finally asked Jennifer.

She looked up, closed the diary, and responded in a thoughtful voice. "It's really not very interesting, but not in a bad way. It's the writing of a fifth- or sixth-grader, so most of it is disconnected thoughts, and sometimes the grammar makes it hard to understand. It's all about ordinary things. But that's what's good. It's fascinating to see 1890 through her eyes. Every now and then, I read her words and can imagine what she's describing and feeling. Let me read you some parts."

Jennifer thumbed slowly through the pages, stopped on one, and read aloud:

> *Dear Diary,*
> *There was a heavy snow today and lots of*
> *people came in the store. I hate big snows*
> *because the people come in and stand next*
> *to the stove and talk, talk, talk!!!! It makes*
> *sweeping the floor harder because they always*
> *have mud on their boots and it smears when*
> *I sweep. I helped make cookies this afternoon*
> *and I did well at it. Matthew took more than*
> *his share and sat in the corner. I wish I had*
> *my own room!!!*

She turned to other pages and read more.

> *Dear Diary,*
> *There was a Negro in the store today. I had*
> *not seen one this close. They are not much*
> *darker than Utes. I do not know what makes*
> *their skin that color. Father says that it is*
> *because of the sun but I am in the sun a lot*

*and I am white. I stayed away from him and
did my chores. There was a young boy maybe
his son. I had nothing to say to him so I did
my chores and did not look at him.*

*Dear Diary,
I hate Matthew!!!*

*Dear Diary,
I think I saw a moose.*

Mogi laughed. "I guess it could have been a moose,
though Ouray's a little south for it. Have you finished the
diary? What was she writing at the end?"

"I'm getting there. Don't be in such a hurry."

"Well, okay," Mogi said, having stood and walked to
the window. "I've got to get out of here or else I'll go
nuts. The rain has stopped. I want a look at Crazy Bill's
cabin. Would you drive me up there? I'll find the cabin
and then I'll jog back. Gotta stay in shape for basketball
because it's no more sitting on the bench for me. I'm
going to be a starter even if I have to practice every day."

"What are you going to do if you find the cabin and
there's a ghost in it?"

"Hmm . . . run back instead of jog."

Jennifer closed the diary, sat up, stretched, and got her
purse. "Okay. While I'm out I'll try the coffee shop downtown. I'll go there after I drop you off."

A half-hour later, as Jennifer drove out of the Thunder
Falls parking lot, Mogi shouldered his daypack and started
up the trail they had hiked the day before. A hundred
yards from the road, the trail curved into a small canyon

and became a series of switchbacks through a forest opposite the waterfall. It was past the switchbacks that the trail leveled out and led to a basin above the canyon.

Having started too quickly, Mogi stopped after only a few minutes to catch his breath.

The pale green grass was up to his knees, small bushes were covered with delicate white flowers, and the trail itself was littered with a wet buildup of the grays, blacks, greens, reds, and yellows of oak and aspen leaves, all mixed with a thick cushion of pine needles.

The early morning rain had brought a sharp chill to the air, as well as a heavy layer of water on the vegetation that was now working its way up through Mogi's socks and jeans. The grass soaked him from the knees down, every bush he brushed against flipped a shower of raindrops onto his jacket, and every breeze shook a new shower over him from the tree branches above. He was glad he had pulled a sweatshirt over his T-shirt and then a jacket over that.

Skirting a clump of oak bushes at the base of a tall Ponderosa pine, Mogi spied another path going left. It was less worn and more narrow. Looking at the shape of the canyon and remembering Nancy's instructions, he guessed that this was Crazy Bill's trail. He turned off and walked at a slower pace, looking carefully at the surrounding forest. He wasn't sure how obvious the cabin would be.

Some minutes later, moving back in the direction of the waterfall and coming into a wider part of the larger canyon, Mogi came up against a thick outcropping of granite. The trail jutted to the right and followed a sharp cut across the face of the outcropping and onto the top. Moving up with large steps, Mogi crested the top as the trail flattened out.

Ahead of him, close to where the outcropping became part of the canyon wall, stood a ramshackle cabin against a cluster of oak bushes. About twice the width of his bedroom at home, it was a small, simple, rectangular building with a roof that sloped to the back. A porch ran the width of the cabin and a smaller roof above it sloped to the front. The porch was wide enough for two rows of firewood with walking room on each side of the door.

Something was funny, and it took a moment for Mogi to realize it.

The cabin was tall. The top of its foundation had to be six or more feet above where he stood. With the height of the cabin walls not much more than seven or eight feet, it made the cabin look out of proportion.

Resisting the impulse to go inside, Mogi walked from one side to the other.

The open space around the cabin was all rocky outcropping. It was not smooth and uniform, like a single layer of stone, but more like a surface of broken shards that had been smashed together, swirled, and then crunched some more so that cracks and crevices ran everywhere. Walking across it would be hard on the toes and ankles. Occasional clumps of grass grew from some cracks while moss and lichen speckled the rough edges and surfaces.

With that as its base, the cabin's foundation was built by laying logs down in Lincoln-log fashion. The bottoms of the first layer of logs had been shaved to match the unevenness of the bumps and cracks of the rock, making the tops of those logs somewhat level. The next logs were then notched in the corners to fit the ones below it, leaving only a narrow opening between the layers of logs.

Mogi counted. To make the foundation that tall had taken almost forty logs. Why did he make it so tall? To keep the cabin above the snow? Seemed reasonable, but it must have been an immense amount of work. At least Crazy Bill had done a good job: The foundation was the one part of the cabin that didn't look old and worn out.

Most of the cabin itself was built of boards, planks, and beams, all looking worn enough to be original. The wavy metal of the roof was new, as was the clouded plastic of the window.

A long, wide stairway in front led from the ground up to the porch. There was an empty doorway at its top, with a single window to its right.

Behind the cabin were remnants of an outhouse. There wasn't much chance of digging a hole in the ground, so Crazy Bill made do with what he had. He simply built a small, flat floor out over a rocky split in the rock going down the side of the outcropping. Putting the outhouse there made the poop hole directly over a fifteen-foot drop. Mogi laughed, not so much from the embarrassment of being so open about going to the bathroom but about how cold it must have been whenever a breeze was blowing up the canyon.

Mogi walked back to the front and up the stairs. A few pieces of newer lumber had replaced worn pieces in the porch. The new wood had not been painted and was already warped. Without someone to clean it off, snow probably drifted onto the porch six months of the year.

Stepping through the doorway, he could see that almost all the rafters had new, smooth wood bolted alongside the old rough-cut originals. The floor was mainly intact, although a few boards were loose in one of the corners.

Mogi sniffed. The air was full of an earthy aroma of dirt and darkness. An ancient table, covered in dust and cobwebs, stood against the right wall under two shelves that had slumped down near the corner. The floor was crusted in layers of dirt, and his running shoes left tread marks wherever he walked.

Old framework between the joists of the ceiling near the back wall was where a stovepipe had gone through. Mogi was sure that no stove had been in the cabin for decades. Woodstoves were valuable, and it was common for them to disappear once a building was abandoned.

To the left of where the stove would have been were the remains of a bed, a rectangular frame with rope crisscrossing from one side to the other, no mattress. Two of the bed legs had given way, so it was more leaning against the back wall than standing. The rope was still intact.

To the right of the door, across from the foot of the bed, were the remains of an old trunk. Its lid had been tossed in the corner, showing its leather straps rotted and barely hanging from the old metal holders. Barely half of the trunk itself still existed. Its sides were scraped, scratched, broken, and dented.

He walked over and peeked inside.

The bottom was covered in wood chips, bark, and pine needles a few inches thick, with a couple of sticks of wood. At some point, someone had used the trunk to hold firewood.

Mogi used the toe of his shoe to lightly kick the base of the trunk, hoping to knock some of the hardened material from the inside. The trunk did not move, which surprised him. Kicking it a little harder, he still couldn't move it, although some of the woody buildup on the inside collapsed to the bottom. Using his hands, he tried to shake the trunk loose, thinking it had become stuck to the floor of the cabin.

It still did not move.

Finally kneeling beside it, Mogi used one of the sticks to scrape a section of crud away from the bottom of the trunk wall.

The trunk had been nailed to the floor.

Mogi laughed. That was pretty smart. Crazy Bill had found a pretty good security measure against anyone who might want to steal his trunk while he was off prospecting.

He stood up, tossed the stick back into the trunk, and walked slowly, methodically around the cabin, looking at the walls, windows, ceiling, dirt, corners, rafters, animal droppings, more dirt, leaves, shelves, table, still more dirt, windowsill, doorway. There was a table, shelves, stove, bed, trunk. Doorway, window, floorboards.

A couple of boards were loose. Mogi pried them up enough to peer underneath. Touching the cross boards, almost touching the floorboards, a solid bed of granite chunks filled the space.

Wow. This guy really did like to work hard. Not only did he build a tall foundation, he even packed it with rocks. No wonder they called him crazy. He must not have wanted any animals crawling under his cabin.

Mogi walked onto the porch and sat down.

Pretty ordinary cabin. Small, but so were the people. The average miner, one of his books had said, wasn't much more than five and a half feet tall. It must have been lonely, especially in a hard winter where the snow could have been three or four feet thick. You couldn't mine in a winter like that, could you? Or maybe you could, if you had dug a mine shaft. The inside of a mine would have probably stayed the same temperature year around, so, okay, maybe you could work a mine in the winter.

Still, when you weren't working, all you had was a pathway through the snow to this itty-bitty cabin, with a woodstove that must have taken truckloads of wood to heat. And a lantern for light.

Those people had to be tough.

Mogi sat quietly, looking at the canyon below and across to the tall peaks. It was quite a sight.

Taking a deep breath, he rose and went back into the cabin. He was remembering the mine exhibit at the museum. The basement had a recreated mine shaft to give visitors a feel for what it was like inside a real mine. It was small and cramped, with sharp edges of rock ready to grab you if you got too close to the sides. You'd never be a miner, Mogi thought, if you couldn't be in tight places.

Giving the tiny house a last review, he glanced at the lid of the trunk in the corner. He walked over and picked it up.

New, the trunk had been a very large, rectangular steamer type. Mogi remembered seeing one like it in the museum. Pretty common in a period when a trunk might be enough to hold all your personal possessions. It wasn't humped like Nancy's small trunk, but had flat sides, bottom, and top. It would have had at least one big drawer unit that lifted out, with lots of little compartments for sorting and storing clothing. The drawer had probably disappeared a long time ago.

The lid had metal guards on each corner, with reinforcing tin running along each edge, though all the metal was now pitted and bent or broken. When new and the lid was shut, two metal clasps hung on the front of the lid and latched into metal slots on the trunk body, and two wide, leather straps were fastened as belts around the whole trunk.

You could put a ton of clothes in one of these, Mogi thought.

He fingered the last, rotted remains of the belts. Only one of the clasps remained.

Mogi looked closely at the clasp. It was a thick, round, flat, metal plate about three inches across, at the end of a short, wide piece of metal serving as the hinge attached to the lid.

Flipping down when the lid was closed, the locking mechanism in the center of the plate clicked into the metal latch below it. The locking mechanism included a keyhole, a small, steel pin centered in the opening. The key to the trunk would have been inserted into the hole, onto the pin, and then turned to lock or unlock the clasp.

It would have been a small key, maybe two inches long, fashioned around a hollow shank.

Mogi was in a full sprint as he shot out the door and off the porch. Picking himself up from a tumble on the still-slick ground, he carefully but quickly ran down the trail and hit the asphalt of the road at full speed.

He was already breathing hard in the cool breeze, but it wasn't from running.

He had just felt the hand of a dead girl.

CHAPTER

J ennifer wasn't at the apartment.

Mogi was bent over, wheezing and gasping, struggling to get more air. Even downhill, running full speed at Ouray's altitude took something out of him.

Jennifer's car was still parked in the apartment's lot, so he guessed that she had walked downtown after dropping him at the waterfall. As he stumbled down the steps and out to the street, he rolled through the possibilities of where she might have gone.

Ah, he remembered—coffee! Jennifer had always been a coffee drinker, and a morning coffee was the one rule she rarely ignored. When she was in a different city, she liked trying different kinds of coffee, especially in little cafes. Bluff wasn't exactly up-to-date with gourmet coffees—it was the Mini-Mart with the gas pumps, the little cafe in the back of the trading post, or brew your own.

Promising himself to keep to a slow trot as he maneuvered around the visitors on the sidewalk downtown, Mogi soon saw Jennifer's ball cap in the midst of the other tourists at The OverFlowing Cup, a popular coffee house with tables outside.

He sprinted the rest of the distance.

Wheezing out his message, he left Jennifer confused as Mogi trotted off toward the newspaper office. Not quite sure what he had said, she understood that he'd run all the way back from the waterfall and now needed her to go back there with him. It sounded pretty serious.

She put a cover on her coffee and set out to get the car.

Mogi had borrowed Nancy's key, run to her house, and was stepping up onto the porch when Jennifer pulled up out front. He wasn't in the house a half-minute before coming out and relocking the door.

Yanking the car door open, he jumped into the seat.

"What in the world is going on?" Jennifer asked in an exasperated voice.

Mogi was still catching his breath as he directed her back to the newspaper office where he dashed in and returned Nancy's house key.

Back in the car on the way back to Thunder Falls, he managed to give Jennifer a description of the cabin—the complete and detailed version ("Good grief—can't you get to the point?") covering the inside, outside, and even the outhouse.

"Okay, okay," Jennifer said, "you've described the cabin to the nth degree. So what are you all excited about?"

"You won't believe what I found if I found what I think I found. But you've gotta see it for yourself."

No amount of prying could get Mogi to say anything else.

Hurrying across the parking lot to the beginning of the trail, Jennifer pulled to a halt and refused to go any farther unless he would at least slow down and wait for her. Half of the pleasure of drinking good coffee was the relaxed time she loved taking to drink it slowly.

"Okay, okay! But you're going to really like this. I mean, big time."

"Well, it'd better be flat-out terrific, dork-boy, or you're going to buy me another coffee."

Finding it less difficult than the first time, Mogi crested the top of the outcropping and staggered toward the cabin. Jennifer was barely to the stairway when he returned triumphantly outside with the broken trunk lid. Sitting beside her on the steps, he pulled a small key from his pocket, the key from Jessica's trunk. Carefully blowing the dirt out of the clasp and wiping the surface, he inserted the key, deftly fitting the hollow shank onto the steel pin, and gave it a turn. They both heard the click of the lock mechanism as the key turned a full circle.

The key worked.

"This very key," he said excitedly to Jennifer as he held it up, "is the key to a large trunk in Crazy Bill's cabin. It is also the key found in a secret hiding place of a twelve-year old girl who was going to vanish within a few hundred feet of the very same cabin. This key is a connection between the two."

Jennifer, still breathing hard from the climb, looked at him.

"This is it? This is the fantastic discovery? You think that this key went to this trunk. Did it not occur to you that this key maybe went to a different trunk?"

"But the key works!"

"That's not what I'm saying. Remember that Jessica's dad ran the mercantile store? They probably sold trunks. At least the store might have had locking cabinets, suitcases, or storage cases for sale. This could be a key to any of those."

"But . . . well, maybe, but it's still a coincidence, right? I mean. . . ."

"And let's not mention that the key was in town at the girl's house when she was vanishing. How many miles is that away from this cabin? And how many years elapsed between her having a key and Crazy Bill actually having used the trunk? I bet there were plenty of these keys floating around.

"And," she went on, "let's assume for your sake that they are the same key. So what?"

Jennifer got up and went into the cabin.

Mogi didn't know what to think. He thought it was a slam-dunk. And it meant that . . . well . . . Mogi wasn't quite sure what it meant—if anything. It didn't help him understand anything about the disappearance, and it didn't seem to tell him any more about Jessica.

The more he thought about it, what Jennifer said seemed more likely. It wasn't that much of a unique key. In fact, he had seen a steamer trunk in the museum that looked like the one in the cabin. The key probably fit it too.

And the idea that the key belonged to a hermit way back in the mountains and somehow had made its way to Jessica's trunk in town? It would have required magic.

Jennifer came back and sat down. Mogi reached for his wallet, removed a five-dollar bill, and handed it to her.

"It's obvious you haven't bought coffee in a nice cafe lately. I want the expensive stuff, a large cup, and a nice pastry to go with it."

"How much more? And you might as well add in the tax."

"Five," she said.

"Good grief! You could get hooked on drugs for less."

"I don't think so, and they wouldn't taste as good anyway."

He gave her another five-dollar bill. "Sorry I brought you up here for nothing."

She smiled. "It wasn't for nothing. I got to see the cabin and made ten bucks at the same time."

They were both silent for a moment. Mogi's lack of a way to connect the girl, the cabin, Crazy Bill, and the key now seemed obvious, besides his looking like a fool. He sat slumped over with his head in his hands.

"Has the diary mentioned Crazy Bill's cabin?" Mogi asked after a moment.

"Nope."

"Has the diary mentioned anything about a trunk?"

"Nope."

"Has the diary mentioned anything about a key?"

"Nope."

"Yeah, okay, well . . . have you even finished the diary yet?"

"Nope."

It was about noon.

"Here's an idea," Jennifer said. "Let's take the lid back to Nancy, show her that the key fits, and see what she thinks. In fact, we could probably get the whole trunk down that trail if we worked at it. We could wash it off and look for writing or something on the inside, and then bring it back tomorrow."

"Well, that would be a nice idea, but it's nailed to the floor."

"It's what?"

"It's nailed to the floor."

"Why would someone nail a trunk to the floor?"

"You're asking me? Why would anybody build a cabin on top of a rock out in the wilderness? I guess Crazy Bill had insecurity issues or something. Anyway, I guess to make sure somebody didn't take the trunk while he was gone, he nailed it to the floor. I'll show you."

Mogi stood up and stretched as he went into the cabin and leaned over what was left of the trunk. Jennifer came up beside him as he pointed to the inside edge where he'd scraped away the dirt and grime. As he did, he noticed the seam of a floor plank.

Kneeling and brushing more of the buildup from the inside edge, he cleared the seam enough that he could see the identical wood as the cabin floor, though much more scarred, scratched, dented, and stained with a thick layer of black wood mold.

He looked at Jennifer. "He *really* didn't want anybody to steal his trunk—he cut the bottom out of it. I guess he thought someone might pull the nails out, so he made the trunk worthless to begin with. Can you imagine the surprise on any thief's face when he saw this?"

Pushing the mess back in place, tossing the lid back in the corner, and feeling disgusted, Mogi left the cabin and hiked down to the car as Jennifer followed in silence.

Nancy met them during her lunch hour, and the three friends walked over to Henry's Sandwich Shoppe.

In spite of the fact that the key fitting Bill's trunk didn't mean anything, Nancy was impressed by what had happened, and couldn't believe no one had ever reported before that the trunk was nailed to the floor.

"How old are you? Are you really a shrewd criminal detective from New York City and only pretending to be a shallow and incompetent Utah teenager? In just two days, you've made discoveries about two completely different stories that happened over a hundred years ago. I can't wait to see what you have by the end of the week."

Mogi grinned as innocently as he could. "I was just lucky with the key, but it could fit any lock like the one on the trunk. And it doesn't help explain anything about the lost children."

"Well, I'm still impressed, and you're going to put the ladies at the museum into shock. They aren't used to hearing new stuff about their old stories."

Lunch was exactly what was needed. Mogi ate with a passion, desperately hungry from his climbing and running. Quickly disposing of a foot-long stuffed sandwich, he attacked a mound of fries with a ferocity that left both Jennifer and Nancy astonished.

"Your dad's wallet must really take a beating," Nancy said as she looked at Jennifer.

"No kidding. And this is mild. You ought to see him after basketball practices."

Nancy left the brother and sister at their car as she walked up the street.

"Well, now what do we do?" Mogi asked.

"We're back at the Corral for supper tonight," Jennifer said. "Then Nancy's going to take us to the mountain slideshow that the chamber of commerce puts on. Tomorrow, Jimmy has tickets for the Durango train, so that'll take all day. I can finish the diary if you'll leave me alone. I see the clouds building again, so my instincts tell me it'll be a great afternoon for a nap. Looks like you're on your own."

"Well, hmm . . . I guess I'll just hang out."

Jennifer left to drive back to the apartment. Mogi looked around for any kind of motivation to do something useful. He found none.

So he wandered. Strolling around the downtown shops, most of which he'd already been in, he went north until he passed the swimming pool—again full of people enjoying the naturally heated water, with as many picnicking in the park next door—then turned and headed back up the street next to the river. Walking the length of the town, which took only a few minutes, he found himself in front of a sign that read "Entrance to Box Canyon Falls."

Interested, he turned, made the hike up to a building, paid a $5 entrance fee, and followed a dirt trail until it became a metal grate walkway.

Hanging from girders attached halfway up the canyon wall, the walkway led through a tall, winding, narrow canyon. There couldn't have been more than twenty or thirty feet between the two walls, but it was a hundred feet high. Scalloped, twisted, sweeping up and around, the walls looked like the curves of frosting on the sides of a cake, smooth and graceful as if a heavenly knife had swirled its way through the rock.

It grew darker as he continued along the walkway, the canyon slowly filling with mist and a thundering noise. At the end, a stairway led Mogi down to the gravel banks of a rushing stream, a few feet in front of a cascading torrent of water crashing into a large pool at the bottom.

The river had cut the canyon, he realized. That's why the walls were so curved and shaped in swirls. It started way out near the valley and carved itself its own canyon.

Close to the bottom of the falls, showered with mist, Mogi's senses were overwhelmed. The roar of the falls dominated all sound. The cold spray of the water covered his face—the wetness was all he could smell—and the pounding of the water shook his whole body. The longer he stood, the worse it got. He couldn't think.

He closed his eyes.

Three children at the bottom of a waterfall. Couldn't hear, see, or think.

Would three children have walked into the falls?

Would they have walked *behind* the falls?

Mogi's eyes jerked open and he fell backward, splaying out on the gravel with his feet sliding into the stream. A couple hurried over to help him up while two kids up on the walkway started laughing.

Red in the face, Mogi struggled up, signaled that he was all right, and moved back to the stairs and up to the walkway, looking off to the side or down or anywhere except at the chuckling boys passing him by.

Still red and sweating from his embarrassment, Mogi was halfway to the entrance before he remembered the image.

Behind the waterfall.

He felt both elated and doomed.

He wasn't sure he could afford all the coffee it would take to get Jennifer back up to Thunder Falls.

CHAPTER

10

"It's not exactly a vote yet," Robin Dubane, the newspaper's reporter, began. "What the corporation wants is a show of support from the leaders of Ouray. If everybody looks like they're in favor, then the corporation will move to the next step and provide an army of lawyers to come in and work out the details. At some point after that, all the details will appear, and then there'll be an official vote. If it goes in their favor, the corporation will draw up a contract, and all we'll have to do is sign and then sit back and count our money."

The topic of conversation in the newspaper office was the same as it had been for months: sell or don't sell. Tim had written articles, Nancy had written articles, and Robin had even written a special series for the Sunday paper. Trying to be fair in their reporting, they presented all the sides, from the millionaires-in-a-day perspective to the living-under-Hitler forecasts.

In spite of it, they were no closer to agreement.

"I wish I could put my finger on my feelings," Nancy said to Robin. "To the marrow of my bones, I feel like this is the wrong thing to do. But I feel it, as opposed to know it. Maybe if this town is to survive for another hundred years, it has to go for the big money and really develop. On the other hand, what's wrong with staying a nice, little town that booms in the summer and sleeps in the winter?"

"Listen, Nancy," Robin replied, "you have to face the facts. If you don't grow, you die. It's that simple. We have no land to spread to, no industry other than tourists, less than a thousand people to pay for the roads, the sewers, the water pipes, and we don't even have enough money to put curbs on every street. This isn't Florida—we're not going to get old, rich people to stay here year-round when they'd freeze their heinies in the winter."

"But what if every street doesn't need curbs?" Nancy shot back. "What if we make do, like Ouray people have done for a hundred years? At the very least, we end up with a town that *we* built, not some international board of directors that treats people like cattle and counts only lift tickets and condo rents."

"Now, you don't know we'd be treated like that," Robin countered. "I expect that everything will be just the way it is, except that our sewer pipes won't freeze in the winter, we'll have better phone service, we'll actually get an internet connection that stays up, it won't be such a struggle for businesses to stay alive, and a lot of people will be very happy. We'll still live here, you know, and we'll keep our identity."

"What identity? You've only been here two years!" Nancy said in a raised voice. "You should have grown up here. Maybe you'd be more worried about waking up one morning, looking in the closet, and seeing nothing but bright, yellow sport shirts with corporate logos sewn on the chest. The marketing department will probably have a little smiley-faced chipmunk that we'll have to put on every brochure in the town and we'll end up hating chipmunks!"

Nancy and Robin had argued like this before. Neither of them expected to win, and it was worse when Tim wasn't around. He was more willing to be neutral. Today, he was over at the mayor's office to talk about the town council. The harder the town leaders pushed for a decision, the more the newspaper-office arguments ended in anger. Nancy always felt bad afterward.

Robin just couldn't see it. She hadn't grown up playing in the backstreets of Ouray, swimming year-round in the pool, hiking the peaks, exploring the mines, seeing the town make it through hard times.

Nancy regretted that her job at the paper didn't involve writing honestly about her feelings so that people could understand her point of view.

The phone rang, and Nancy answered it. Tim was asking her to walk across the street to the mayor's office. She stalked out, already assuming it wasn't going to be a good meeting.

Montgomery Harrison, the Millennium Corporation's director of planning and design, sat casually in a chair next to the mayor's desk. As Nancy came in, he rose, reintroduced himself, and sat down. He continued talking to the mayor and Tim.

"It's my opinion that it would help the whole town of Ouray if the leadership were seen as being of one mind. The newspaper is an important influence on the town's thinking, as well as an interpreter of the leadership's mind. If you have a leadership that speaks with one voice and a newspaper that supports that voice, you'll have a town that follows its leaders. If you have a newspaper that can't reflect the thoughts of the town leaders and doesn't provide the words needed to direct people's minds in the right direction, then your townspeople will be like lost sheep.

"In short, I would like to give you, the mayor and highest elected public official, access to Millennium's considerable resources in the information arena. We will be happy, as soon as you pave the way, to make available professionally written articles to help the citizens of Ouray correctly understand the situation and see the true leadership their mayor is providing.

"It would also," he said as he glanced at Nancy and Tim, "improve the newspaper considerably. I'm sure the townspeople would like that."

Nancy was stunned. She looked at Tim, who looked back at her with an expression of defeat.

"I thought you ought to know what was being talked about," Tim said in an apologetic voice.

Drawing himself to an upright position, leaning forward and placing his arms on the desk, the mayor looked at Nancy.

"Nancy, it's time for leadership. Not namby-pamby, can't-make-up-our-minds leadership like we're used to but leadership that understands what choices need to be made for the future of the town and everyone in it. Now, I've been talking with Mr. Harrison ...."

Nancy drew her chair noisily across the floor and put it directly next to Harrison's. Ignoring the mayor, she sat, put her hands on the chair arms, and leaned forward until she was only inches from his eyes.

"Let me see if I understand what I believe you're saying," she began in a firm voice.

"What you want to do is take over the only neutral source of information in town so you can brainwash the general populace into accepting the corporation's offer. You want to present only positive information about the offer and to prevent the communication of any negative information about the offer, thereby controlling public information for your own benefit."

If the Millenniumn's director of planning and design had had any blood, he might have blushed. As it was, he looked directly into Nancy's eyes, turned to look at the mayor, and then returned to Nancy.

"I believe that we will have sacrificed the idea of a free press," Nancy continued.

Harrison's lips drew tight. With a slight tilting of the head so his eyes now looked down at her, he spoke with an even voice.

"Free press is a joke. Even with your present newspaper, what gets printed is what the writers write and what the editor edits and what the advertisers advertise. You don't print just anything; you have policies and standards. And those standards dictate that you follow certain guidelines about what is said, how it is said, and when it is said. You have, no doubt, in the past done what every newspaper person has done before—you left something out, or you discreetly put it on the last page so most people would miss it.

"What I am suggesting is that you stop pretending to know everything, and print what your leaders tell you to print. They will tell the people what's right to do, and the company will help put it in the right words. You print what's given to you. If you can't handle that, you should strongly consider who will be paying your salary."

Nancy grew red with anger. She hated manipulation in whatever form it took, and could see the deliberate workings of a very large and forceful institution that was willing to cheat to guarantee a win. She especially hated when it was excused as "the right thing to do."

She spoke very carefully.

"I guess I had misunderstood about the newspaper representing the community, rather than the leadership. I always thought people had the right to think for themselves." She leaned back in her chair.

Montgomery Harrison never took his eyes from hers and never blinked. Like a snake.

"You have to tell people what to think," he continued. "They actually prefer it most of the time," he said matter-of-factly. He moved his gaze back to the mayor, who was dumbfounded as he watched the confrontation.

Harrison gave a little smirk and added forcefully, "I believe I was correct in my assessment of the situation. It looks like we have someone who's not a team player, your honor."

Nancy thought about strangling him, but the death would be too quick and painless. Instead, she stood up, replaced the chair, and walked toward the door.

She paused there, turned around, and spoke in a calm, firm voice: "I quit."

Turning on her heel, she walked from the room, crossed the street, went back to her office, closed the door, and cried, shaking with frustration, embarrassment, discouragement, and fear.

CHAPTER

J ennifer walked to a large boulder away from the cascade of rocks at the foot of Thunder Falls and sat, her head leaning to one side as she watched her brother.

Skirting around the rocks and boulders, carefully moving his feet from one slick surface to the next, Mogi went as close to the rock wall on the right as he could, struggling to work his way behind the cascading torrent of water. He was soaked in a few seconds. He finally retreated, circled around as far left as he could, and tried the same thing. Same results.

Frustrated, he tried a full assault on the water, running as hard as he could straight into it. Like a few thousand sledgehammers, the water pounded him down and pushed him across several large rocks. Picking himself up and grimacing as the water stung his shoulders and back, he made his way down the rock pile and up the bluff to where Jennifer sat.

Soaked and shaking from the cold, his bony chest showing through his shirt and his knees bloody from encounters with the rocks, Mogi plopped down next to her with a dejected look. After a minute or so, he looked at her.

"That really hurt. That water must be going a hundred miles an hour."

Jennifer stood and helped him to his feet, then they walked back to the car. She made him strip to his underwear and wring out his clothes before getting in, as well as put a towel from the trunk over his seat.

Mogi said nothing as he reached into the console, retrieved his wallet, removed a ten-dollar bill, and handed it to her. She smiled and tucked it into her pocket. He felt fortunate to have gotten away so cheaply.

Back at the apartment, as Jennifer walked to the bedroom to resume her nap, she turned and looked at him.

"You seem to be working really hard today at guessing wrong. Maybe you need a time-out."

She shut the door.

Mogi changed into dry clothes and stared out the window. Maybe I do need a time-out, he thought.

He grabbed a drink from the refrigerator, left the apartment, and walked down the street to the museum.

"Excuse me. I wonder if you have any more information on the Crazy Bill legend other than what I found in the history books?" he asked.

The woman at the desk was willing to help. Yes, there might be something more, she said, and started shuffling busily through a file cabinet behind the counter.

"We try to keep all the records together, especially if we've provided any information for books or magazines, or to newspapers," she said. Moving from one drawer to the next, the woman finally pulled out a manila folder and laid it on the desk.

"Let's see what we have," she said as she opened it and spread out the contents. There were a few papers, several newspaper articles (some very old), a picture of the cabin, pages torn from magazines, and a discolored pamphlet.

"Okay, this is probably the best source we have." She pushed the pamphlet toward him.

"In 1899," she said, "for the New Year's celebration of the new century, the Ladies Auxiliary put together a series of pamphlets on the history of Ouray. They gathered up all the stories, legends, eyewitness accounts to incidents at the mines, and anything else they could think of. There was one for the history of individual mining companies, one for the businesses in the late 1800s, one for the houses of the rich, one for legends and mysteries, and a couple of others. They sold the pamphlets for a nickel apiece to buy fireworks. This particular pamphlet includes a first-source account of what happened to Crazy Bill. Most of the information in your history book came from here, but the pamphlet has some details that weren't included."

Mogi gingerly opened the little book and carefully thumbed the pages until he came to the section titled, "The Mysterious Death at Thunder Falls."

The following is from an interview with Harold MacKinnon, an early resident of Ouray:

It was in the fall of 1881 that we found the body.

They say his name was William Jenkins, but nobody called him anything but Crazy Bill. He seemed not to mind. The place was pretty wild when he first came in the '70s, but the gold fever hadn't hit yet, so it wasn't the wild of people. The old man had panned for gold for most of the recent years, but finally settled down and built himself a cabin up Thunder Canyon.

Not many people knew him and he liked it that way. Refused any kind of help in building his cabin, didn't like visitors, and only made it into town once or twice a season though it was less than a morning's ride. Didn't like people, I guess. He was peculiar. Always paid for his supplies with dust. Even paid for his whiskey with gold dust. Don't remember a mine, though, so he must have been panning.

It was his mule that told us something was wrong. Crazy Bill had bought a mule from the stables north of town. The stables was where they put together mule trains for the mines way up in the mountains, sometimes putting together a hundred or more mules to bring the ore down to the crusher in town. These mules got used to it, you see, so the owners'd lead them up to the mines, load them with ore sacks, and then point them down the trail. They'd come right back to the stable. Didn't have to drive them or watch over them or anything.

Well, Bill's mule came loping into town one day and headed straight for the stables. It was an awful sight—hide and bone. Hadn't been fed for some time. This made me and the sheriff wonder about old Bill. We mounted up to go have a look.

When we got to the cabin, we was pretty sure something was wrong. The rails on the corral were broken, figuring that's how the mule got out, and the cabin door was closed. We called for him but got no answer, so we went through the door.

God Almighty, I had never been much of a churchgoer but I started that day. It was the look on his face that chilled me to the bone. He was lying close to the table, stretched and twisted, with his hands all splayed out and crooked, and his whole body was knotted up like a raw nerve. But his face! His eyes were bulging wide open, blood had shot out of his ears and nose, his lips were drawn back into an awful grin, his tongue was all swelled up, and everything made it look like he was in the middle of a scream!

I'm no coward, mind you, but my heart was pounding and my stomach was twisting. The sheriff looked around but decided that we needed Doc to come up before we moved anything. I offered to go back to town and fetch him.

When we came back, even Doc started sweating at the sight. He couldn't find anything wrong. No broken bones, no bullet holes, no bumped head, no bites, or anything. He said it didn't look like poison. More like he had been scared to death.

Yeah—scared to death! That's the way he looked!

We hauled the body to town. There was a minor discussion of which side of the cemetery fence to bury him on but he was finally laid to rest proper.

We nailed the door shut to keep the animals out and tried to find a family to notify. Didn't seem to be, so we let it go. Over the next few years, there were some stories about dead animals on the porch and some kids came back with a story of seeing Crazy Bill's ghost, but I don't put stock in it.

It wasn't until after those children were lost that people started having a real fear. There was something unnatural about the place. Whenever I went up to check on the cabin, I'd never hear birds. Over the years, I heard more stories about ghosts and voices and about people hearing the crying of children, but never heard them myself.

I wonder about the children. It was unnatural, too, them disappearing and all.

Some people say Crazy Bill's ghost was lonely and wanted company. I don't know.

The museum lady was kind enough to make him a copy of the story. Mogi thanked her and walked back to the apartment, taking his time, mulling over the details.

He quietly opened the door and sat at the desk in the corner of the living room. After silently moving the papers and magazines to the floor, he found a pad of paper and set it in the center of the desk.

It's a gift, his mother told him, being able to remember things so well. He didn't consider it a photographic memory because he could also remember all the times when he had forgotten something. But it was unusual—if he saw something, he could pretty well bring the image back into his mind, and if he heard something, or read something, he could almost repeat the words.

It made taking tests great, but the downside was that his brain sometimes got too full. It was up to him to sort it all out and figure what was important.

Taking his pen in hand, he asked himself a simple question: What do I know about the lost children?

1. Three children vanish from a picnic on August 19, 1891. Two girls, one boy, 10 to 12 years old. Jessica, Matthew Jacobson, Margaret Thayer. Daughter and son of a storeowner. Daughter of a banker.
2. Big search effort—lots of people over several days; nothing found.
3. Disappeared in a canyon with a waterfall. Close to a cabin where an old miner died 10 years before, in 1881. Supposed to be haunted. Some strange stories over the years.
4. Cabin has a chair, table, shelves, stove, bed, trunk. The trunk lid has a lock.
5. Jessica's trunk has a secret bottom with a key, diary, baby blanket, and doll. The key fits the latch of the cabin's trunk but may have been a universal key for that kind of latch.

Mogi kept writing, now adding questions about the facts.

1. Crazy Bill's body was horribly disfigured when they found it. He was discovered by way of his mule escaping and coming to town. Can anyone really be scared to death?

2. Cabin has one door, one window, tall foundation of logs, wooden floor, rocks under the floor, shelves, no stove but had one. Around the corner from the waterfalls, built on a rock, outhouse on one side over a cliff. What happened to the stove? Where'd the rocks under the floor come from?

3. Trunk is nailed to the floor, bottom cut out, recently used for firewood, lid is in the corner, leather belts are broken and worn, one latch is gone, but the remaining clasp is metal, big with a keyhole that takes a key with a hollow shaft. What did he keep in the trunk? Why did he nail it to the floor? Why did he cut out the bottom? Where did he keep the key?

4. Crazy Bill was a gold panner and paid for his supplies with gold dust. Did he have a mine too? Where would it have been?

5. Had Jessica been to Bill's cabin?

The bedroom door opened behind him. Jennifer stretched and wandered over to the desk. She peered over his shoulder at the lists.

"I finished the diary," she said. "You're going to need more paper."

CHAPTER

12

Mogi pulled the desk chair next to the window as Jennifer curled up in the armchair and spread the diary open on her lap.

"Okay, if you'll be patient with my slow way of doing things, I'll go back a little from the last entries of the diary. I marked some places. She has this dated May 20, 1891. That's about three months before she disappeared."

> *Dear Diary,*
> *Today we picnicked at the falls and I have a really big secret!!! I cannot believe this has happened to me!!! I wish I could tell somebody but I do not dare because no one could keep a secret like this and I promised myself that I would not tell anybody not Matthew not Mother not Father not anyone!!!*

"I'll skip a few days because she doesn't mention the secret or the falls again. There's a page dated July 5. Something happened the day before, so she must have gone on another picnic, like maybe a Fourth of July celebration. Notice how the tone has changed. It's also longer, which is unusual for her."

Dear Diary,
I do not know what to do. Maggie keeps telling
me to tell Mother or Father, but I just cannot.
We were not to be there at all. I was so afraid
when she went down and I started crying and
I wish that I had not. It was my secret and she
should not have gone because I told her not to
go but she did and I was alone and wanted her
to come back. I yelled and yelled.

Mogi interrupted.

"Maggie is Margaret Thayer, the other girl that was lost, right? Do you have any idea of where she's talking about when she said 'went down' and 'I was alone'? It seems like it fits being at the falls. They must have been at the bottom of Thunder Falls, like where I climbed down to the rocks."

Jennifer thought for a moment. "I don't have a clue. Maybe they were climbing down to the bottom of the waterfall, like you say, but that doesn't seem as scary as what she's describing."

I yelled and yelled. She started daring me and
I would have none of it! She is not going to be
my friend anymore!!! I wish I had never told
her my secret!!!

"Doesn't sound like the falls. Remember how noisy it was, and how wet you got? They wouldn't have been able to yell at each other, much less go unnoticed."

Mogi leaned back in his chair and put his hands behind his head.

"Now, let me go to three days before the day they disappeared," Jennifer said.

"Before you do that," Mogi interrupted, "I have a question. Why doesn't she tell what the secret is? I mean, in her diary. Why does she call it a secret instead of writing the secret itself?"

"Oh, if you had ever kept a diary, you'd know the answer," Jennifer said. "A diary is a special place for your innermost thoughts, until you figure out that your mother could find it and read it. It's an ever-present danger.

"So, you write everything until you get down to the very details and then you have a certain number of words, like 'secret,' 'special place,' 'special friend,' 'most important happening in my life,' et cetera, that you use in place of what you're really talking about.

"God forbid you should ever write the name of your crush in your diary. Your best friend might read it and then where would you be? Understand?"

Mogi shrugged. "Well, no, but I'll take your word for it. I can admit, though, that I've never, ever drawn a map to my ruin back home. That ruin I discovered in the canyon near Bluff is a special place, and I wouldn't risk anybody invading it."

"You probably do understand, then. Okay, listen some more. This is August 16. Remember they disappeared August 19."

> *Dear Diary,*
> *Maggie keeps telling me that she is going to*
> *tell the secret to everybody!!! I hate her!!! I am*
> *hoping that there will be a big rainstorm and*
> *nobody will get to go. At least she cannot get in*
> *without me!!! IT'S MY SECRET!!!*

"That's the last entry. Three days later, they left the picnic and ran into the woods, never to be seen again."

"I don't understand," Mogi said. "She has a secret. She reveals it to her friend Maggie, so Maggie becomes a major player, which Jessica then regrets. Maybe this is leading to blackmail?"

He wrote a couple of sentences on his notes.

"Maybe the 'climbing down' was into a cave behind the waterfall?" He didn't want to give up on the waterfall idea.

"Or maybe it was a small canyon, or a cut in the rock, or they were 'up' before she 'climbed down,' like in a tree house or something.

"What do you think?" he asked Jennifer.

"I'm out of my league. You're the one who's good at sorting through stuff like this. But what I *feel*, what I think *she's* feeling, is that whenever the secret was first discovered, nobody knew about it but her, not her parents, not her friends. She was scared of them finding out, because, I would guess, it was a place or action or thing that she wasn't supposed to be at or do or have.

"Too excited to keep it in and wishing, hoping, for the kind of friend that she really values, she finally tells her friend Maggie. Right after that, in the July 5 entry, Maggie apparently did something related to the secret that upset Jessica a lot. At that point, Maggie must know what Jessica knows and Jessica now hates that she told Maggie at all.

"I suppose," Jennifer said, "that other people finding out wasn't as much the problem as the fact that Jessie wasn't going to be the one to reveal it. This really ticks her off. It was her secret—she should get to tell it if it has to be told. I think Jessie knew she'd eventually have to tell somebody, someday, but she wanted it to be on her own timetable.

"What's most interesting is the last phrase—'she cannot get in without me.' That's a power-struggle statement. That's the phrase that makes me think she expects to force Maggie to follow her will. But I'm stumped as to what it was."

Mogi jumped a foot when the phone rang. It was Jimmy. Jennifer answered, talked for a few minutes, and hung up with a worried look.

"Nancy's not going to supper or the slideshow. Jimmy didn't go into detail, but things got bad enough at the newspaper that she quit."

Mogi's eyebrows shot up. "Quit? You mean like outta-work-type quit?"

Jennifer nodded her head.

"Is she at home?"

"I think so. Jimmy said she wanted to be alone. He said we should meet him at the Corral whenever we're ready for supper."

Mogi thought for a minute. "Well . . . that's pretty interesting. Should we do something?" he asked her.

Jennifer looked at him, and he could almost hear her thoughts.

"I believe I'll go for a drive after supper," she said with a grim face. "I may drop in at Nancy's while I'm out."

It was late when Mogi came back to the desk, staring at the loose pages of notes. Supper was nice, but both he and Jennifer had been preoccupied, and even Jimmy didn't have much to add. Jennifer had dropped Mogi off at the apartment and left for Nancy's.

He read through the last pages of the diary.

This was the most important stuff, he thought. It had to be. Jessica was almost there, almost to the picnic, almost to the point of when she and the others vanished. If there was any explanation of what was going on the day of the picnic, then the last entries had to reveal what was going on.

What did it all mean—the "climbing down" and the "secret"—and especially the "she cannot get in without me"?

He leaned his elbows on the desk, cupped his chin in his hands, and stared harder at his papers. There was a lot of information. Jessica's diary, the story about Crazy Bill, the story about the children ....

Mogi got his camera and browsed through the photos.

The cemetery, the angels and the plaque, a picture of Nancy's house, the puppies, and the small trunk. Several pictures of the museum and the statue. The pictures of Thunder Falls, the old cabin, the remains of the trunk—one with the key on top of the lid, and another showing the nails along the bottom. A few more of Box Canyon Falls. Then several more from the bottom of Thunder Falls.

He straightened the pages of facts and questions and placed them on the left side of the desk. The Ouray history book went at the top and he laid his notebook in the center.

Slowly, methodically, he looked at every piece of information relating to the three children, moving them from left to right across the desk. He was sure he had the information that could tell him the whole story: who did what, and when, and why. All he had to do was get everything in the right order and then listen to what it was saying.

CHAPTER

"I might as well come along. Suddenly I have lots of free time on my hands," Nancy said.

Jennifer did not leave Nancy's house until well after midnight, making a 5 a.m. departure difficult for both of them. The group needed to be at the train station in Durango by 6:45 to make the 7 o'clock train.

She and Nancy were trying to nap in the back of the Jeep, but even with the soft-top covering that Jimmy had added, the noise of the wind and tires made sleeping impossible. Mogi watched the mists swirling along the ground in the headlights as Jimmy did his best to keep the Jeep under the speed limit.

Driving high into the mountains, they left the morning mist behind and were soon enjoying the sun as it highlighted the rugged peaks. As they wound through narrow corridors of rugged peaks and thick forests, they dropped into a layer of thicker clouds as they passed through Silverton and then climbed back up to weaker sunlight.

The people must have been extraordinary, Mogi thought, to live and work in places like Silverton and Ouray. From the top of Mount Sneffels, looking down at the old mines, it seemed too rugged, too hard, too remote for any kind of regular life. How would anybody do it?

But people *did* do it. They came and they stayed. A lot of them. All over the mountains, and the valleys too. Silverton, Ouray, Telluride. Even the people in Durango were bound by heart and hand to the mountains and the mines.

It had to be about more than money.

Within an hour, coming down out of the mountains, as they passed the Purgatory ski area and glided down a long, sloping highway, the mist returned and the sky was overcast. They still had several hours before a storm was due to move in. Forecast as only a minor disturbance, it was still expected to bring rain and wind.

Having reached the train station and bought their tickets, they found their seats in one of the antique passenger railcars. Mogi and Jimmy took one of the padded bench seats, and Jennifer and Nancy sat in front of them.

Mogi was jolted back in his seat as he heard a thunderous hiss, followed by a series of loud whistles. A large, black plume belched from the locomotive's smokestack, followed by smaller puffs of smoke shooting into the air as periodic jerks ran up and down the railway cars. The train started out of the station.

A genuine, fire-breathing, chug-a-chug-a steam locomotive pulled the coal tender, seven passenger cars, a boxcar, and a caboose through the center of Durango and up the valley floor for several miles, then patiently chugged its way up into the Animas River canyon high in the San Juan Mountains. To make the elevation change of more than a thousand feet and still have a small enough grade for the locomotive to successfully climb, the train track had been carved out of the side of the almost-perpendicular valley walls, providing spectacular views of the canyon.

After twisting and turning through the Animas Valley, the train would pull into the ancient mining town of Silverton, turn around, and repeat the trip in the opposite direction. Going both ways took all morning and afternoon.

Mogi stuck his head out the window and looked at the river below, photographing as much of the canyon as he could.

The Animas River, broad and flat in the wide canyon at the foot of the peaks higher up, narrowed into channels of watery fury as it poured into the steep gorges leading to the valley below, creating waterfalls that plummeted a hundred feet or more and crashed into the riverbed with a rumbling like an earthquake.

He had never seen anything like it.

A mile after the falls, the track leveled off so that the train steamed next to the river. Winding back and forth across it, the railway moved to whichever side of the river had enough flat land to hold the track.

In the middle of the canyon, the train stopped for a large group of backpackers to get off, retrieving their packs and equipment from the boxcar. Intending to hike for several days in and around the basins and peaks, they'd return to the track afterward and be picked up by another train on its return trip to Durango.

The remaining ride to Silverton was less dramatic but still beautiful. The narrow canyon gave way to a wider river, more valley floor, and huge forests of aspens. Finally exiting the valley, the train pulled directly into downtown Silverton. The passengers hustled off and swelled into the streets.

The train backed itself onto a spur track, turned around, and backed into the town on the same rail as before, ready to start the return trip after lunch.

After a quick meal, Nancy led her friends on a short hike to the Christ of the Mountains shrine. On the side of a steep slope west of Silverton, it took almost twenty minutes to climb the steep path. Though it looked small from the town, the shrine was a fifteen-foot, solid marble statue of Jesus, his arms outstretched to the expanse of valley below, embracing the town and the surrounding land.

"This is really something," Jimmy said, staring up at the figure.

"It was commissioned and built in a time when the town was not doing very well," Mogi said. He was half-reading the bronze plaque at the bottom, half-recalling from the train booklet. "The townspeople hoped the shrine would bring them good luck. The year after it was built, the town was revived by a new mining operation, so people attributed the good fortune to the shrine.

"It was rededicated a few years later after the town's deliverance from a catastrophic mine accident. An entire lake broke through its bottom into a mine shaft and flooded miles of tunnels. Had it been on a regular day, hundreds of miners would have been drowned. As it was, it happened on a Sunday morning, and not a life was lost."

He looked up at the outstretched arms. "Just like he was taking care of them."

Nancy moved away from the base of the statue and sat on a small wall in front. The little town below was dwarfed by the expanse of rocky peaks above it. The remains of mines dotted the sides of the mountains from one end of the valley to the other, with old cable lines for ore buckets, large buildings where the ore was crushed and sorted, and the common cone-shaped piles of mine tailings.

Mogi sat next to her.

"Look at the valley from the left and follow it all the way to the right," Nancy said. "I bet there're two dozen mines. I can't imagine the number of people who lived in this valley when all the mines were producing."

"I remember the mine tailings we could see from Sneffels," Mogi said. "What amazes me is how hard it must have been to dig those holes into the solid rock. If I was doing it, I would have stuck with working the rivers with a gold pan."

"Me too," Nancy replied. "Getting the rock out of a tunnel, loading it up, hauling it to some place that could crush it and get the gold out—it must have taken forever unless you could afford a huge operation."

"So Crazy Bill probably just got his gold from the streams. He may have never even had a tunnel."

"I expect," Nancy answered. "There were never any tailings found in Thunder Canyon, so unless he had a mine way up in the basin, he probably had a sluice box in a stream somewhere. I've always wondered if it might actually be in the river that turns into the waterfall. Heck of a climb, but it drains a good portion of the mountain basins up there."

They heard the train whistle in the distance. Nancy stood up.

"That's the return whistle, so we've got about twenty minutes to make it back to the train. We'd better hurry."

The trip back was relaxing and fun. Having experienced the scenery riding up, Jennifer sat in the rear seat with her brother and watched the people. Most of the young kids were drifting off for afternoon naps, as were some of the older passengers. The young couples with children, their kids asleep, were perched on the seats with arms and elbows on the windowsills, enjoying the view.

There was a cafe car near the middle of the train where coffee, soft drinks, and snacks were available. Most of the teen-age passengers busied themselves walking back and forth through the cars.

Mogi slumped in the corner of his seat, leaning against the window as he looked out and wondered about the country.

Moving equipment and belongings from one place to another, building towns that went bust, moving to build in another town, always having to go up and over the rugged mountains. Working small claims, working for big companies, working the rivers and streams in one valley, then another. Working deep mines, going in and out every day, dirty, exhausted, nothing much to look forward to.

Relentless, he thought. That's the word. Life must have been relentless.

The rhythm of the train was relaxing, almost hypnotizing. The massive wheels click-clacked on the rails with a slow cadence, and the huff-puffing of the locomotive was like background music. It was cool and comfortable, and the rocking of the train jerked mildly like a rocking chair with uneven rockers.

Mogi zipped his jacket up around his chin and closed his eyes. The click-clack of the wheels kept on with soothing regularity.

There was the desk, the papers and pictures in front of him. The story was there—all he had to do was listen. His mind drifted:

A hard-rock prospector with a loaded mule moves along a path in the mountains. Steadily moving up a rocky trail. No one else for miles. The high mountains, the afternoon rain showers. Cold, lonely, hard. The prospector trudges forward under granite spires.

The train is there, small towns, large mines. Big crushers churn out smoke and dust. From the top of Sneffels, people move about far below in a constant flow. Like little ants moving in and out of big holes in the rock walls.

There's a ruin back in one of the canyons close to the cabin, a sandy floor enclosed by tall walls of sandstone, high up among the old stone homes of the Anasazi Indians. A place to get away from everyone, a place where he can think. He's sitting. His head is back, resting on the wall.

A click-clacking rhythm echoes around the walls. He floats up the sandstone walls and there's Sneffels and then Thunder Falls, with people, all sorts of people, dressed in Victorian clothes, laughing, eating, picnicking, and playing games. The smell of the food is strong and delicious as it lures everyone to the tables while the waterfall crashes with a thunderous roar onto large boulders, drowning the surrounding trees in a constant mist. It's a happy scene, a picture of family, of town, of people celebrating.

There's an old cabin on a tall foundation and three children climbing a trail toward it. Two girls and a boy. The two girls argue about something. One of them doesn't want to go, but the boy is eager and is out front, leading the way, joining with the one girl to taunt the other.

The unwilling girl has a small key but does not let the other girl see it. But the unwilling girl doesn't have the key anymore, because it's in a trunk back home. That's why they can't get in. She won't let them. The tall one screams, It's my secret! The children go into the cabin without opening the door because there is no door.

They don't come out.

An old man lingers on the porch, smiling, holding out a hand that's covered with gold dust. The man is smiling. A big smile that gets bigger and bigger, ear to ear, and his teeth grow large until it turns his face into a grimace, a face of terror, a mask of horror. His eyes bulge out, straining. Blood shoots out his ears and nose. His body twists even more.

Scared to death.

The children don't come out.

Other people are climbing the trail, calling out names, looking around the trees, going into the cabin, coming out of the cabin, calling out names, carrying torches, looking all around, looking into mine shafts, calling out names.

But the children don't come out.

And someone is screaming, screaming, screaming, screaming.

Mogi woke up with a start.

The rhythm of the train came back; the clicking of the wheels made him remember. His fatigue was replaced by sadness. Deep, intense sadness. He sat up, took a deep breath, and looked at Jennifer.

"I know where the children are. I know why they were never found." His voice caught in his throat, and he turned away.

Jennifer focused on him, suddenly unsure whether she really wanted to know. What if the answer to the mystery brought grief instead of closure? But she did want to know.

"Can you tell me?" she asked in a gentle voice.

Mogi took a deep breath. "I need a little time to get the whole picture together, so hang with me for a while."

He gave a small laugh. "I already owe you for two goofed-up ideas. I can't afford another one. That fancy coffee is pretty expensive."

Jennifer smiled back and leaned her head back, and they shouldered together into the softness of the seat.

It had been more than a hundred years. There was no need to hurry.

CHAPTER

14

Mogi was silent on the ride back to Ouray, going over the whole story in his mind. It all made sense. Simple, really. But he needed, really needed, to know if he was right.

There was only one way to know—he had to go where the children went.

The storm was moving in as the Jeep passed the Durango city limits. Wind, light rain, and lightning in the valley. It rained harder as they passed the ski area, and Silverton was shrouded in clouds as they went down to the town and then back up again as the highway climbed out of the valley to cross over the mountains. Red Mountain Pass, between Silverton and Ouray, had enough snow to cover the highway.

It was almost eight in the evening when they got back to town. Coming down from the high mountain passes, the snow changed back into a rain and sleet combination driven by wind gusts. It was as if the town had been pressed down by a blanket of wet darkness. As dinner plans were discussed, the rain slacked off to a light drizzle that whipped into little swirls under the streetlights. They picked a pizza place in the center of town.

Warm and cozy inside the small shop, they felt a mood completely different from the other nights. Jennifer was anxious to hear what her brother had discovered, but it was harder for Nancy and Jimmy to believe that the youthful teen-ager had figured anything out. Jennifer assured them it would be worth waiting for; she'd seen it before.

Finally, Mogi started talking.

"I'm about to tell you a story. I made it up, but I think it's close to the truth."

They all leaned forward, elbows on the table.

"Around 1880, there was an old trapper who had a secret. This secret was the location of a gold mine. Whether he started digging and found gold, or if a natural opening was already there, I don't know. Whatever it was, having found it, he was determined that no one else should know about it. So, to hide the mine, he did a clever thing—he built his cabin right on top of the mine entrance.

"To get into the mine, he created a trapdoor in the floor of the cabin but needed to hide it as well. So he cut out the bottom of a large trunk and made a trapdoor that fit in the opening. Then he nailed the trunk around the trapdoor.

"To go into the mine, he opened the trunk, opened the trapdoor, and went down. When he wasn't in the mine, he simply closed the trapdoor and shut the lid on the trunk. When he was away from the cabin, he probably filled the trunk with something, like blankets or books or equipment."

Three people at the table looked stunned.

"You mean, for all these years, there's been a mine under that cabin?" Jimmy asked, not believing.

"That's why you can see the floor boards inside the trunk. The trapdoor must fit the bottom almost exactly so you don't see the seam. I was looking at it, but I didn't see what I was looking at."

"You're making this up," Nancy said. "I hate to be a skeptic, but there's not a mine there. It's been a hundred years. Somebody would have found it by now."

"If the cabin had been occupied right after Crazy Bill's death, probably so. But the cabin was abandoned; the cabin door was even nailed shut for some time until somebody stole the door. And, even after that, with all the stories of ghosts, I bet nobody went near it for a long time. It could have sat for years without being used. By the time somebody did stay in it, and used the trunk to hold firewood, nobody was thinking in terms of any mine that Crazy Bill had.

"You actually gave me the important piece to the puzzle," Mogi said as he looked at Nancy.

"Me? I didn't do anything."

"Remember at the shrine? We looked at the mines in the valley. We recognized them because of the junk rock—the mine tailings—spilled around the entrances. If Crazy Bill had had a mine, there would have been tailings. That's why everybody thought if he did have one, it had to be outside the canyon. But what if he could *hide* the tailings instead of dumping them out front?

"That's why the cabin has such a tall foundation. He built it so he could hide the tailings under the floor. I expect he pulled up the floorboards, filled the space underneath with whatever he dug out of the mine, and then replaced the boards. That's why I found the space under the floor full of broken rock. He did have a mine, and he did have tailings—you just couldn't see them."

The others were still shaking their heads and furrowing their brows, so he went on.

"Let's go to ten years after Crazy Bill died. Sometime in May, Jessica Jacobson and her family go on an outing to Thunder Falls. The father plays with the boy while the mother gets the picnic ready. Maybe there are other families. But the twelve-year-old daughter goes exploring. I bet you ten to one that she knew about Crazy Bill's cabin and was strictly forbidden to go near it. But this time, maybe for the first time, she disobeys.

"She goes to the cabin and goes inside. If the cabin had been as ignored as we think, it's probably in good shape, including the trunk. She looks around, explores a bit, and discovers an old key. I don't know how or where.

"Maybe the trunk was closed and locked, or closed and unlocked. Either way, she discovers that the key fits the lock on the trunk. That simple connection makes her pay attention to the trunk.

"By some action, she finds that the bottom of the trunk opens. Maybe she crawled in the trunk playing an imaginary game of hide and seek. Maybe she was fascinated with the size of the trunk and stepped into it. Maybe she was exploring the floor of the trunk for a hidden panel, just like the one she had made for her own trunk at home. She steps into the trunk and the bottom moves. It opens enough to show her that it's a trapdoor. She opens it and stares in disbelief, but I bet she does not go down into the hole. After a while, excited beyond anything she's ever felt before, she closes the trunk and, ten to one, she locks it."

Mogi looked into three pairs of eyes. "And now she has a secret. She can't tell her parents because she wasn't supposed to be in the cabin in the first place. She struggles with telling her best friend, so much so that she doesn't tell her right away. So the key goes into her hiding place and she keeps the secret to herself. But she does write about it in her diary. That's the May entry.

"Now, it's the Fourth of July celebration, and the family makes another trip to Thunder Falls for a picnic. By this time, Jessica has told Maggie, and they both go to the cabin to see what Jessica found. Jessica does not expect Maggie to climb down into the mine, but she does. Jessica's furious and mad and lonely and resentful. That matches the diary entry that talks about 'going down' and 'all alone.' And afterward, Maggie has Jessica's secret and uses it like blackmail in their relationship.

"So that sets the stage for the August picnic. All three children now go to the cabin, but Jessica thinks she can control the situation because she left the key back at her house, in the false bottom of her small trunk. She expects that they won't be able to open Crazy Bill's trunk without the key, so they won't be able to open the trapdoor. That gives the power back to Jessica. But something happens and the trunk is opened, and, for some reason, all three children go down into the mine.

"I'm just guessing here, but something bad happens and the trapdoor shuts and can't be opened from below. They're stuck. Nobody back at the picnic has a clue about the mine or the trunk. Even when the cabin is searched, it looks completely empty.

"That's where the children went, why they were never found, and it's still where they are."

Nancy leaned forward. "You know, I still think this is pretty fantastic. Are you sure you're not way off base? A hundred years! Generations of people who have never heard of Crazy Bill have been in that cabin. Every single one of them missed it?"

"Well," Mogi responded, "I may be absolutely, completely, without a doubt, dead wrong in everything that I've guessed. All I've done is create a story that takes everything we know—the key, the children, the legends, the cabin, the diary—and makes it all fit together."

He hesitated.

"In this case, however, we have a way to test it." He paused and looked at his friends. "We can go to the cabin tonight and see if that trunk is the secret entrance to a mine."

They were all silent.

Finishing the pizza quickly, they left the cafe, got into the Wrangler, and took off up Main Street. None of them noticed that the Jeep was not the only vehicle to suddenly come to life. About five seconds after it left, a large, black Chevy Suburban with two men inside pulled out from a side street, accelerating in the same direction.

CHAPTER

15

They stopped at Nancy's and Jimmy's houses to get clothes for hiking, heavier jackets, and flashlights. Jimmy also brought his camping lantern. Then they drove to Thunder Canyon and started up the winding road to the falls.

The storm had increased to a steady rain, and strong gusts of wind whipped down the canyon. Every few minutes, a bolt of lightning crackled across the bottom of the clouds. A few seconds later, working its way up and echoing off the canyon walls, a thunderclap would boom above them like a volley of cannon.

The Jeep shook in the gusts, the soft covering snapping against the rollbar. If they had wanted a night for adventure, this one was giving them more than they bargained for.

"That's funny," Jimmy said.

"What?" Mogi replied, swaying back and forth in his seat to match the Jeep's movement along the curves in the road.

"It's a crummy night to be out, for sure, and we're nuts enough to be here. But we're not the only ones. There's somebody behind us."

The three others turned and looked down the road. Every now and then, on an outside curve, headlights flashed through the rain.

"Remember that little side road ahead?" Nancy said quickly. "Pull into it and turn your lights off."

Jimmy gave a quick glance behind him, peered ahead to find the road, turned in, pulled ahead about thirty yards, and doused the lights. Then he pulled on the emergency brake so the car would be stopped without the brake lights shining as they would with his foot on the pedal. They all sat in silence, turned in their seats, watching the road.

A half-minute later, a large, black Suburban passed like a shadow.

Jennifer felt a violent shiver run up her back. Nancy felt her shake.

"You okay?"

"I just had another one of those feelings," Jennifer said. "I had one yesterday." She paused. "Somebody's in danger, and I think it's us."

Leaning their heads together, they discussed what to do. Before they could reach a decision, the SUV whipped by again, headed in the opposite direction. A minute later, Jimmy backed the Jeep onto the pavement and sped up the road. They parked next to the picnic tables, which seemed safer than leaving the Jeep next to the cabin trail.

After a tense, hurried, and wet hike, Jimmy turned the lantern on in the cabin as the others began to clean out the inside of the trunk. On impulse, they gathered the leaves, pine needles, bark, and dirt and put them into the trunk lid.

Mogi ran his finger slowly around the inside edge, looking for a handhold or fingerhold to pull up on the bottom. He found none. He tried the knife trick that Nancy had used on the false floor of the small trunk. Nothing moved.

Jimmy tried it, then the others. It wouldn't budge.

Mogi sat back. "It has to open! If this were a real mine, there would be rock, tools, buckets, all sorts of stuff going in and out of the entrance. It had to be easy to open or it would have been useless." He sat and thought for a minute.

"Wait. Here's an idea." Mogi moved to the side of the trunk. "We've presumed the trapdoor is opened by pulling up. Maybe we need to push it down instead." He pressed his hand directly on the middle of the floor. Nothing moved. He moved his hand to the left side and pushed again. Nothing. To the right. Nothing again. To the top, to the bottom. Nothing moved.

The wind howled outside, scattering rain through the open doorway. The roof over the porch rattled and banged against the wood rafters.

"After a hundred years, maybe it's just stuck." With that, Jimmy stood and put his foot in the trunk and stomped hard on the center. Nothing. He followed Mogi's pattern—middle, left side, right side. . . .

The trunk floor rose an inch and slammed back down.

"Oh my gosh!" Jimmy stomped again on the right side of the trunk bottom. The left side went up an inch and fell back. He did it again, this time harder. The left side rose two inches and fell back.

"There must be some sort of rod across the bottom," Jennifer said, "and the trapdoor rotates on the rod. When you step on the right side, it causes the floor to rise up. If you can get it up far enough, we can grab it with our hands."

The level of excitement and adrenaline skyrocketed. It *was* a trapdoor!

The harder Jimmy stomped, the higher the floor came up. There was a loud screech as metal scraped on metal. Finally, the floor, now a door, came up enough that Mogi and Nancy could grab it. They held it until Jimmy could also get a hand on it and then all pulled together.

The trapdoor slowly wrenched up with an awful scraping sound and was pulled back against the end of the trunk. Underneath, a metal pipe attached to the bottom of the floor planks was wedged into two metal brackets, forming a hinge. Jennifer had been right.

They all peered down.

From the cabin floor through the floor joists onto the rock below, Crazy Bill had built a boxed-in shaft, maybe six or seven feet long. Past the bottom of the shaft, they could see a rough, ragged rock opening. A small breeze came out of the hole, sending shivers through the four young people staring down.

"Rats. What we need is a rope to use to lower the lantern," Mogi said.

Jimmy moved toward the bed. "I believe we can take a few liberties here," he said as he began unraveling its strands of rope, cutting through the knots he couldn't untie. Removing ten feet or so, Jimmy tied the lantern to one end and lowered it into the hole.

Through the wood sides and past the rock opening, the shaft went straight down about ten feet, then angled away toward the cliff. Along the edge of the shaft, small holes had been chiseled into the rock.

"There are steps when you get to the rock," Mogi said, pointing to them. "But how do we get down the wooden part?"

The four of them examined the boxed-in part. It was built out of rough-cut lumber stacked on edge, attached to corner planks that ran vertically. But the sides were smooth and unmarked except for two fist-sized holes on the narrow side below the hinge.

"You think he had a ladder?" Nancy suggested.

"Good guess," Jimmy said. "Imagine coming up with a bucket of broken rock. He'd have to have something more than just footholds."

"I think I'm tall enough to get to the rock," Mogi said. "Let me try. Maybe there's something below that will help."

Leaving the lantern at the level of the rock opening, Mogi was about to step over the trunk sides when he stopped.

"I forgot," he said, as he opened his daypack, rummaged around, and pulled out a ball of string. "This will make sure we don't go anywhere we can't get back from." He tied the string to the metal rod, dropped the ball of string into the hole, and climbed back into the entrance.

Holding onto the trunk sides as long as he could, using the opposite side boards to keep pressure against his body, he lowered himself until his outstretched foot caught the rock. From there, it was easy to use the footholds.

Taking the lantern, he immediately found the answer to how Crazy Bill had gotten past the opening box. A well-used ladder lay on an incline of dirt. The rungs seemed to be okay, but the tops of the rails were split and twisted, and one leg was broken off about a foot from the bottom. On the dirt, Mogi noticed two metal staves that had been bent in a U-shape.

Handing up what was left of the ladder, their use became apparent. The bent staves at the top had been bolted to the rails of the ladder. The staves were inserted in the two fist-sized holes in the wood. Held in place, the ladder presented a sturdy platform to go through the trapdoor.

Not having the staves to secure the ladder, Mogi held onto the bottom of the ladder and kept it steady as Jimmy came down.

Holding the lantern in front, the two walked or slid down an incline, a sort of ramp, for about fifteen feet. As the ceiling leveled off, the shaft opened up in height. About twenty feet from the bottom of the entrance shaft, they found themselves in a large room, the ceiling several feet above their heads.

"It's a cave!" Mogi said. Holding the lantern high, he glanced around the room. There were several buckets, shovels, picks, and a few boxes. It looked like a storeroom.

"Let's fix the ladder so the girls can come down," Mogi said. Having Jennifer throw down another length of rope, he grabbed a pick and tied the handle alongside the broken rail. Putting it back in position, he tested the ladder and then told Jennifer to be careful.

Going back to Jimmy, he flashed a light around the walls, ceiling, and floor.

Across the chamber was an entrance to a tunnel. It was not natural like the cave but had been chiseled out with tools and gunpowder. As they prepared to go down, they heard a commotion behind them. A light bounced around the entrance.

Jennifer hit the ground at the top of the ramp.

"Somebody's coming!" she said in a loud whisper, then caught the daypacks Nancy dropped from above.

Mogi and Jimmy quickly moved to Jennifer's side.

Jennifer made a shushing sound. Nancy was above them, halfway down the ladder, trying to quietly pull the trapdoor down after her. Slowly, slowly, she inched it down. It took almost all her weight to make it move. Whenever a squeak of the hinge started, she stopped. She knew she couldn't wait long, so she started again. The squeak was louder.

Mogi opened his pack, took out a water bottle, stepped up the ladder, and passed the bottle up to her. She squirted water onto the pipe, then pulled again. The squeaking became a muffled grind, and she pulled the trapdoor until her hand was pinned in the crack. Struggling to get her fingers into a better position, she immediately stopped as the sound of boots hit the porch outside. She slipped her fingers through.

The four of them froze.

The heavy thuds made by hard-heeled boots came through the cabin's doorway. Another set of sounds joined the other. There were brief flashes of light through the crack of the trapdoor. Nancy felt her arms quiver as she expected a shout from above.

The lights moved on.

Jimmy had turned off the lantern and the flashlights, plunging everything beneath the trapdoor into absolute darkness. Muffled voices spoke above them, then moved outside. Whoever it was had crossed out onto the porch, and their footsteps were heard no more.

Jennifer turned on her flashlight, covering it with her hand. Mogi slowly lowered himself back down the ladder, followed by Nancy. Sliding down to the flat floor of the cavern, the four of them collapsed on the ground. After waiting a few minutes more, Jimmy turned the lantern back on.

"We thought we heard a car come into the parking lot, making us think that maybe the SUV was back," Nancy said, whispering. "I spread the leaves and stuff back around the trunk and slid the lid back into the corner. Just as I was getting down through the trunk, I saw a flashlight beam on the trail. Thank goodness you thought about squirting water on the pipe! I thought we would be caught, for sure. Do you think they know we're down here?"

Everyone had an opinion, but the consensus was that the two people above didn't know where they were and were just searching blindly. They might have followed the tracks in the muddy trail, but the rocky outcropping in the rain would have shown no trace of them.

"Who do you think it was?" Jimmy asked.

Nancy said, "It's got something to do with the Millennium Corporation. It has to. I think they're after me."

"Maybe they just want to know where you are," Jennifer said. "I can't imagine they'd do anything. Maybe they want to keep up with you until they get their contract signed." The girls talked about it for a minute more, ending with little more clarity than they had started with.

The four continued to explore the cave. Mogi held the lantern above everyone's heads and turned slowly around to see. Suddenly, he froze.

From the tunnel entrance ahead came a long, low moan.

CHAPTER

16

"What was that?" Jennifer asked.

After clearing his throat from a sudden dryness, Jimmy answered, "Everybody, uh, relax. That's not unusual for a mine. When I took my first mine tour, the same thing happened. If there's a lot of wood reinforcing the tunnels, it will creak as the temperature changes. Wind blowing across the entrance to a mine will also do it. If there are multiple tunnels in a mine, the wind moving in and out of the tunnels sets up vibrations too, like organ pipes or something."

"Oh, good. That gives me options other than the ghost of Crazy Bill coming to suck the life out of me," Jennifer said as she tried to smile.

The moan faded away. Everyone stood still, half-expecting another surprise. Cautiously, Mogi gave Jimmy the lantern and swung his flashlight beam around the room.

"This is a natural cave," Mogi said slowly, thinking as he spoke. "Crazy Bill must have stumbled across the entrance, come down, looked around, and figured he could carry on a mining operation without anybody knowing about it. He builds the cabin, makes the trapdoor, and now he can mine to his heart's content without fear that someone will jump his claim. Pretty clever."

Mogi focused his flashlight on the tools on the floor. A hundred years, he thought, exactly like Crazy Bill had left it the day he died. He leaned closer and wiped the dust from the top of a wooden box.

Dynamite.

He took a picture, the flash bursting into the darkness like fireworks.

"There's a box of dynamite over here," he called to the others, pointing it out. "I suspect it's safe as it is, but I wouldn't go playing with it."

He continued around the room. Jimmy found a metal hook jammed into the ceiling and hung the lantern from it.

Mogi picked up the ball of string, made a loop around one of the picks leaning against the wall, and stepped to the opening of the tunnel they had found. Jimmy moved to go with him and Jennifer checked her watch, asking them to be back within twenty minutes.

Leaving the lantern suspended in the large room and training their flashlights in front of them, Mogi and Jimmy moved into the rocky hole. Their voices and lights faded into the darkness.

Nancy moved closer to the ramp and focused her flashlight on the walls and ceiling. "Mogi was right. This ceiling is completely natural. The walls too, although there are shelves cut into them every so often. They must have been used to hold candles or lanterns."

Jennifer looked at the piles of stuff. Shovels and picks stood together, the boxes were lined up with each other, and the lanterns hung together on a peg. Even if he was crazy, she thought, the man had a sense of order. She checked the names printed on the sides.

Where did he buy his supplies? Did anyone wonder about his buying all of this stuff when he didn't have a mine?

Jennifer walked to the other side of the cave, her light trained on the floor. Spying something against the roughness of the rock, she bent down and picked up a partially burned candle. It was the only one she had seen in the chamber. With the lanterns around, candles must have been kept for emergencies.

It was a minute or two before the return time for Mogi and Jimmy that lights flashed from the tunnel's entrance and the two boys walked back into the cave.

"It wasn't as deep as we thought," Mogi said. "We found another shaft that veered to the left about thirty yards from here. We checked out the right tunnel to the end and then came back. Who wants to go back and see where the left one goes?"

"You can count me out," Nancy volunteered. "This is far enough for me. I'm not exactly claustrophobic, but that tunnel looks awfully small."

Jimmy added that he was more used to being on the tops of mountains instead of inside them, and volunteered to stay with Nancy.

"How about you?" Mogi asked his sister.

"Me? You want me to go into a tunnel the size of a dragon's nostril? I'm pretty happy here."

"No, you aren't," Mogi said with a smile and gently tugged on Jennifer's jacket as they both walked into the tunnel. Running gradually downward, the main tunnel curved slightly to the left. They came to the branch tunnel in a few seconds and stopped, tying onto the string that ran to the right. Within the next fifty yards, the new shaft curved harder to the left. Without an outside reference point and with only flashlights, it was hard to tell how far they had come. It still sloped down.

Jennifer reached forward and brought Mogi to a halt.

"Listen," she said. There was a low, deep sound, a kind of rumbling. "What is it?" she asked Mogi. He listened for a minute and then put his ear against the wall. It was a constant pounding, a pulsing sort of sound.

"Duh, it's the waterfall!" Jennifer exclaimed. "Think about the location of the cabin. From directly below it, we've probably moved left through the outcropping about a hundred yards. That puts us pretty close to Thunder Falls."

Mogi nodded. "I think you're right. Now here's a question: Why would Crazy Bill go in this direction, instead of back into the mountain? This rock is the same outcropping. If he hadn't found gold or silver yet, you'd think he wouldn't waste time tunneling through more of it."

Mogi crept forward, cautiously, shining his flashlight up and down and around and forward, the light dancing like a nervous firefly. He grew more wary as the sound grew louder, and felt a shaking beneath his feet. The walls of the tunnel were dripping with water, and small puddles appeared on the floor.

Fifty feet more and the dull noise had grown to a thunderous roar. Mogi entered another, larger room, where the tunnel took a sudden, sharp turn to the left. Shining his flashlight to the left, he saw a sheet of fast moving water in front of them.

Thunder Falls.

CHAPTER

17

The roar was too loud for them to talk. They did a quick inspection of the rock-hewn tunnel. There was an old wheelbarrow, a pick, a coil of disintegrated rope, and a few lanterns. The equipment, walls, and floor were covered with a thick layer of moss and slime. It was a steam room but cold instead of hot, the spray of the cascading sheets of water filling the tunnel with more water than air.

Mogi tied his string to the wheelbarrow, breaking the ball off and putting it his pocket. There wasn't much left.

Swinging her light around as she stepped forward, Jennifer felt something against her boot. Bending down, she was again mystified to find a single candle lying in a puddle, caked with moss, an inch or so longer than the first. She carefully looked across the floor but found no others.

Mogi, knowing they were late, motioned to Jennifer, and they left the chamber. He continued to inspect the tunnel on the way back but moved quickly. Jimmy and Nancy were sitting on the ramp.

Mogi described what they had found.

"I thought that Crazy Bill took his broken rock and put it under the floor of his cabin. He did, but under the floor wasn't going to be enough space for everything, so he used that space for whatever he needed until he could cut a tunnel to behind the waterfall. After that, he could dump as much stuff as he wanted. Since the bottom of the falls is all rocks anyway, no one would ever notice.

"From the looks of it, he spent his time tunneling to the waterfall. We've only found one more partial tunnel. If that's the case, he didn't spend much time finding any gold or silver. He still must have gotten his spending money from panning the rivers."

The length of the day showed in their faces. More exploration would have to be left for another time. They gathered their packs, moved up the entrance, pushed open the trapdoor—slowly at first to check for any signs of the men who'd followed them—and climbed out the trunk. They tried to smear dust around to camouflage their boot marks on the floor, but it didn't work too well, so they walked around the cabin several times to make more tracks in other places.

The storm had become a light, steady rain, and the wind was gone. Everyone was quiet until they were once again in the comfort of the Jeep.

"What we need is a couple hundred feet of those waterproof lights and a generator," Jimmy said. "String those babies down there and we can really see everything. We need a geologist too so we can find out if there's any gold or silver. Some of the guys that work at the Hummingbird mine north of town come into the Corral sometimes. I bet I could ask them for some equipment. Plus, they'd probably take care of that box of dynamite."

Pulling up in front of her house, Nancy leaned forward. "I have a favor to ask of all of you," she said. "I want you to not do anything about the mine. At least not yet. Give me tomorrow to get a plan going to deal with my problems with the newspaper. Don't mention the cabin to anyone, and we'll see what the situation is tomorrow night. I think I can use the information to an advantage if we use it at the right time."

Jennifer looked toward her and caught her eyes.

"Does this have something to do with the Millennium Corporation?"

Nancy gave her a small smile. "I can't stand by and watch everything I've grown up with become a playground for the rich and famous. I refuse to be intimidated by a bunch of jerks. And finding this mine only emphasizes what a special place this is.

"If you're willing, I need all of you to help me tomorrow. I'm starting my own newspaper."

*   *   *

It was after midnight before Mogi and the others made it to the apartment. Nancy had not explained her idea, leaving it to a meeting in the morning, ten o'clock sharp. Mogi fell onto the couch and immediately wormed his way into his sleeping bag.

Outside, as the last light blinked off in the window, a man in a black Suburban parked in the alleyway made a phone call. A few seconds later, the black beast sped off into the night.

Back to Thunder Canyon.

Exhausted in every part of his body, Mogi tried to sleep but couldn't close his eyes. He had put all his energy into discovering the trapdoor and the mine, and hadn't thought much beyond it. Now having confirmed all he had guessed, he wanted to feel righteous, accomplished, like a king after a victorious battle. Instead, he didn't feel much at all. He was numb.

Finding the mine wasn't enough. He had wanted to find the children. That was the real mystery.

Jennifer sat on the side of the bed feeling the same crazy feelings—victorious and disappointed at the same time. The last puzzle piece hadn't been found. The small trunk, the diary, the key, the cabin, the big trunk, the trapdoor, the mine—all those pieces fit together.

But no lost children.

Jennifer remained tied to Jessie. The diary had brought her into the world of a twelve-year-old girl—young, innocent, open, honest. Feeling part like a friend, part like a big sister, and part like a mother, Jennifer desperately wanted to find her.

The last piece of the puzzle.

A few hours later, the day arrived with a dull light that barely made the difference between night and morning. The storm had settled into the valley, making a ceiling of clouds that extended halfway down the mountainsides above the quiet village. No rain fell, the air was calm and heavy with moisture and coolness.

Jennifer thought she was being absolutely quiet, but Mogi rose up from the couch and looked at her as she came into the living room. They both knew that given any noise less than a bomb going off, Jimmy would sleep until noon.

Breathing deeply and stretching his tired muscles, Mogi stood and put on his clothes. He added a sweatshirt—he would need it to keep the chill of the mine from his bones.

They moved quickly, gathering the lantern, flashlights, extra batteries, water bottles, string, paper and pencils, and snacks for breakfast. Jennifer wrote a quick note to Jimmy and put it next to the bathroom sink.

They were a mile up Thunder Canyon before Jennifer spoke.

"I need to talk about the children again," she said. "Now that we know there's a mine under the cabin, I want to see if I can add to the story."

Mogi yawned. "Okay, but my ideas of what the children did are even more guesswork than finding the mine."

Jennifer nodded. "I agree," she began, "that in the May visit, Jessie found the key and the trapdoor but didn't go down. This was the secret she first wrote about in her diary. Some time later, she told Maggie Thayer. Either way, she kept the key.

"On the next visit, the two girls snuck away and went to the cabin. Jessie took the key, opened the trunk, and showed the trapdoor to her best friend. Unable to stop her, Jessie watched Maggie climb down, probably only to the bottom of the ladder. They had no light, so she wouldn't have gone far. I agree with you that that's when Jessie writes that she was yelling down at her while she's alone at the top.

"The next time the two girls were there would have been the day they disappeared. Jessie expects to control the situation by not bringing the key, but I bet that Maggie messes things up. She probably gets really mad at Jessie, gets a rock or something, and pops the lock open. Or maybe she had found another key. However she did it, Maggie came to go into the mine and she's not about to be denied. And I think she's the one who brought these." Jennifer dug around in the bottom of her daypack and held out the two candles. "I found one of these on the floor of the big cave and one at the waterfall."

Mogi wondered how he had missed them.

"When Maggie goes down into the mine, not having been stopped by the lack of a key, Jessie doesn't have a choice. She has to go down, too."

"How do you figure Matthew got involved?" Mogi asked.

"I think he was just being an annoying little brother who wouldn't go away, like most little brothers," she said, eyeing Mogi knowingly. "Sometimes they can be the rottenest little creatures. Anyway, he may have discovered their plan before they went on the picnic, or, suspecting something was about to happen, just wouldn't leave them alone."

"What then?" Mogi asked.

"After what we found last night, I think the ladder broke. Crazy Bill would never have left it at the bottom, so it had to happen after he was dead. I think all three children were on the ladder, it pulled out of the metal hooks, and they all fell into the shaft. And when the metal pulled out, it was so close to the hinge that it caused the trapdoor to fall."

"You know, you're really good at this," Mogi said. "So now we have three little kids stuck in the mine. Nobody knows they're there; nobody even knows the mine is there.

"They're in a heck of a mess," he continued. "They try to get the ladder back up but can't get it to work. They can't crawl up the wooden part without it because there're no footholds.

"They scream for help, for sure, but it could have been several hours before anyone was looking for them. And even then, if someone entered the cabin, they would have given it a quick look-over and left. The cabin, truthfully, was completely empty."

"Mogi," Jennifer began, glancing at him briefly as she watched the road, "we missed something yesterday. I know they're down there, just like you knew the trunk covered a trapdoor. We missed them. They were there and we missed them." Tears came to her eyes. "Thanks for coming and putting up with me. I know it's safer to wait until we bring in a cast of thousands to search the place." Jennifer turned to him and added, "But I wanted us to do it first."

As she returned her eyes to the road and rounded a corner, she barely had time to jump on the brake and swerve to a full stop.

Across the road were several wooden barriers and orange barrels, the kind used in road construction. Behind the barriers, a backhoe was working at moving a large pile of dirt from the road, scooping it up and dumping it into the back of a truck. A man in a hardhat, carrying a clipboard and wearing a yellow reflective vest, walked over to their car.

"You're going to have to turn around. There was a big mudslide last night, so the road's closed for a while."

Mogi couldn't believe it. There was no mudslide last night! He leaned over toward the man outside Jennifer's window.

"Uh," he began, "how long is it going to be before the road is open again?"

The man bent down and looked at the two teen-agers. "The pavement was damaged by rocks and debris, and it looks like it may have washed away some of the roadbed. It may be a couple of weeks or so, maybe longer." The man gave a little smile, shrugged his shoulders, and walked back to the barriers.

The two of them sat stunned. As Jennifer turned the car around, Mogi glanced up the road. Parked off to the side, half-hidden by another bend, was a black Suburban. It looked like the same SUV that had followed them the night before.

CHAPTER
18

Mogi slapped Nancy's breakfast table with his hand. "There wasn't a mudslide on that road last night! It had stopped raining by the time we left. Somebody is faking that mudslide to keep us from getting back to the cabin!"

Mogi was bleary-eyed and exhausted. The others looked as bad.

"Keeping us from the cabin doesn't make any sense," Nancy said. "Nobody knows about the mine. Why would they care?"

Nancy's comment brought Mogi up short.

"Besides," she added. "You saw the SUV up the road from the mudslide, right?"

"Well, yeah," Mogi replied.

"It just happened to be up at the falls before the slide happened? No way! It's me they're after. They're making fun of me because I won't play their game. They're showing that they can control what I do and where I go, and they don't know anything about the cabin. But it doesn't matter anyway because they're hounding me to stay put and out of their hair. They think they can treat me like a little girl, and I'm not going to stand for it!"

The last sentence slammed into the air as Mogi pulled back from the table and slumped against the chair back. He wasn't part of the conversation anymore, and that was okay with him.

Nancy paced back and forth across the dining room.

"I'm going on the offensive. If I can get through to the people of the community in a big way, then we'll run those guys in the SUV right out of town! I've written some stuff that's going to make the Millennium Corporation pay for what they're doing, and they'll regret ever coming to this town!" Nancy's voice was cold and mean.

Jimmy hunkered down in his chair.

Mogi didn't understand. The problem yesterday had been the mine. And the children. Today it was the Millennium Corporation. But he wasn't done with the mine! He wanted to focus on the kids, not some dumb company. Why was Nancy suddenly forgetting everything from yesterday?

"This is my plan," Nancy went on. "I've already called the newspaper office in Montrose. They've helped us out in the past when our press was broken. They'll print a special run of whatever I come up with, but they need it by two o'clock to get it out by tonight.

"I got up early this morning and wrote enough copy for a single, newspaper-size page, printed on both sides. Cut in half and folded, it gives us an eight-page, half-size special edition. I doubt we can do this every day, but I'm planning on at least two editions a week, even if I have to paste in a lot of pictures.

"I figure there're at least a couple of weeks before the mayor's crowd will move for a vote, so I'll have five or six direct hits on their ship. Having a competing newspaper will be enough to light a fire under the sheep of this town and make them sit up and notice what's happening.

"I would love to see Montgomery Harrison's face when he sees what I'm doing. I'm going to rip his head off!" Nancy was almost snarling.

"We have to get the layout ready, but that won't take as long as you might think. I've got the computer file from a special, half-size Christmas issue we did last year. We'll take that, plug in my stuff, and be ready to go. Jimmy already knows the software, so it'll go pretty quickly.

"When it's ready, Jimmy and I will take it up to Montrose and run three hundred copies. We'll be back after supper, and then I know people who'll help us pass it around town."

There was no more discussion about the mine or the children or the mudslide or anything. Mogi was mad. Didn't she understand the priority? He almost had the whole story about the children. They couldn't stop now!

But he didn't have a choice. With the activities of the day laid out by Nancy, there was no option but to go along.

Jennifer helped lay out the paper, Jimmy and Mogi worked on the electronic file, and Nancy made phone calls or visits to people around town. She raised enough money for the first issue and started spreading word about the conversation she'd had with Harrison and the mayor.

She made it sound as bad as she could.

Nancy rewrote some of her pieces about the corporation's proposal into a single article. She added a short story on what it felt like to be thrown out of her job and a medium-sized piece about individual liberty, the right of people to think for themselves, and the place of a free press in America. On almost every page was a large banner that blasted the Millennium Corporation.

Jennifer was stunned. Every other sentence was filled with angry words, every paragraph hot with accusations, every story describing the Millennium Corporation as a foul and hideous monster set to ravage the very soul of the community. Nancy even reported the recent "landslide" on the Thunder Canyon road. Every incident was interpreted as a defiant manipulation of the town to get a successful endorsement for the corporation's offer.

The discovery of the mine was not mentioned.

"Uh, Nancy," Jennifer said as her friend raced out the door on another errand. "Are you sure you want to do this?"

Nancy brought her face close to Jennifer's. "I'm going to have my pound of flesh," she said. "Montgomery Harrison is going to regret ever having met me!" She turned and walked away.

Jennifer's face was red. She tried remembering her place. She was helping because Nancy had asked her to help. It wasn't her role to create the newspaper, and Nancy had far more invested in the town than she, a tourist from Utah.

The tone of the articles bothered Mogi too, though it wasn't his fight either. Even Jimmy grimaced as he read them. A public hanging was fun at first, but in the end, it felt embarrassing.

"She's really hot about this. I've never seen her after blood before," Jimmy confided to his cousins. "I'm not sure this special issue is going to go over too well. She'll look silly if she keeps it up.

"I hate to say it, but something bad is going to happen."

CHAPTER

19

Mogi leaned back in his chair and closed his eyes. He hurt all over.

His watch showed a little before 2 in the afternoon. Nancy and Jimmy had already left. Munching on the leftover crust of a take-out pizza, Mogi and Jennifer quietly sat at Nancy's table.

"Do you think the Millennium Corporation is as bad as she says?" Mogi asked.

"Even if they are bullies," Jennifer replied, "she's making them out to be worse than the mafia. I personally think it's only that jerk of a planning director. He knows that Nancy is a long-term resident and has a lot of influence over the townspeople. I'm sure he wants to keep her muzzled, but I think she's gone overboard. She's really, really angry."

"I hope she gets over it," Mogi said. "I'm glad I'm on her side; she'd be a bad enemy. Anyway, I've thought a lot about this morning and decided that the roadblock is good news and bad news."

"Tell me the bad news first."

"Well, the bad news is that they blocked the road. That means we can't get to the cabin, which ticks me off a lot.

"The good news is that they don't know it's the cabin we're going to. If they did, they would have boarded up the doorway, or blown it up, or something else to keep us from going inside. So they don't know about the cabin and they especially don't know about the mine.

"It's also good news that, with the mudslide in place, they're watching Nancy and not the two of us. So if they don't know we want to get to the cabin, and they're not watching us, then they won't be expecting us to go there by the back way."

He had added the last sentence with raised eyebrows and a smile.

"What back way?"

"Well," he started hesitantly, "I want a chance to look for the children before the mine is made public. You do too. I thought that since you got me out of bed early this morning, I could probably talk you into taking the other road to the cabin."

"There is no other road to the cabin," Jennifer said with a puzzled look.

"Well, actually, there is, uh, kind of."

"I'm lost. Fill me in on this other road."

Mogi took some keys from his pocket and threw them on the table.

"Okay," Jennifer said, "I see the keys to Jimmy's Wrangler, since he went with Nancy in her car. So what?"

"Well," Mogi started.

"Wait a minute," Jennifer's eyebrows shot up. "You're not thinking what I think you're thinking, are you?"

Mogi took a map out of his pocket. It was Jimmy's trail map from Mount Sneffels—showing all the trails and backcountry jeeping roads in the area.

"Oh, good grief! You are not even *suggesting* that I drive a Jeep trail, are you?"

"What's a Jeep trail? Just a road without asphalt. The Jeep does all the work."

He opened the map and traced a winding route across the tops of the mountains to the basin above the cabin.

"What are you scared of? Look at the trail on this map. We go back up the highway between Ouray and Silverton about three miles. The trail is clearly marked. It goes off to the east and up and across a basin or two before it gets to the mountain above Thunder Canyon. And look, here's the hiking trail we were on the first time we were there. We know we can do it because we did most of it the other day. All we have to do is drive a little piece of the Jeep road, then hike down the path to Crazy Bill's cabin. Piece of cake."

"Piece of cake? Are you nuts? Do you remember how far down the mountain we would have slid the other day if the Jeep hadn't gotten hung up? Like a fast drop to certain death? Do you remember the rocks bounding down the mountain at a hundred miles an hour? You're crazy if you think I'm going to drive a Jeep trail."

*   *   *

The Jeep's transmission let out a constant whine as the low gear caused the tires to thrash against the rocky road it was climbing. They drove up through a canyon of trees out onto a narrow path across the face of a mountainside, and up and over a pass that seemed higher than some of the peaks around it.

"We're gonna die!"

"No, we're not going to die," Mogi said. "I'm good at reading maps, the accelerator's on the right, the brake in the middle, the clutch on the left, and there's this stick-thingie you use to shift gears. Everything's normal, and you're doing fine."

"We're gonna die!".

With the lack of sleep from the night before, Mogi and Jennifer were quickly running out of energy, making the constant jerking and jarring of the wheels crawling over the rocky path hard on their nerve and spirit. Jennifer had given up trying to shift the manual transmission without grinding the gears and had just left it in a gear low enough to creep up every steep part of the road. Mogi figured that was good enough, though slow, and he turned his attention ahead, his hands holding the map against the Wrangler's dashboard. The details were accurate and the trail was easier to follow than they'd expected, though several sections of road featured a sheer dropoff on Mogi's side. ("Don't you dare close your eyes!")

It was almost five before they crawled to a stop in a high basin. Looking to the north and west, they could see the familiar granite faces of the cliffs west of Ouray.

"Okay, this is it, I think. We should be able to walk down to the left and find the trail that goes to the cabin," Mogi said.

Jennifer pushed her body off the seat and finally stood on solid ground. She raised her arms to stretch her tight muscles, bent around in a full circle, and let her arms fall to her side. She sighed.

"You cannot even imagine how much coffee this is going to cost you. You may need to buy a franchise."

They were just under a layer of clouds, making it darker than normal for late afternoon. Struggling to put on his pack, making sure they had the lantern and flashlights, the weary brother followed the weary sister down the mountain to the canyon below.

*　*　*

"I think the lantern will give us a couple hours of light," Mogi said. "Along with fresh batteries, we should have lots of time to look around."

Mogi strained to pull the trapdoor open, lowered the two backpacks down the hole using the rope from the night before, and then lowered the lantern. He used more rope from the bed to tie the trapdoor to the bed frame. He was more frightened of the door accidentally closing on them than the men from Millennium.

Having smelled it before, he was much less bothered by the cave's heavy odors. Following him down the incline, Jennifer went to the center of the cave and stood still.

"I thought about this a lot last night, and I want to try something," she said. "Turn off the lantern."

Mogi wasn't quite sure about this, but he obeyed his sister. Not using their flashlights, they stood in the cave with only a little light coming through the trapdoor. Their eyes slowly adjusted to the dark. Mogi heard a match being struck.

Jennifer lit the two candles.

"This is what they saw," she said quietly.

The light coming through the trapdoor was dim from the darkness of the overcast sky. There were no harsh shadows from the lantern or flashlights, and the candles gave the cave a surprising amount of light. As the two teens' eyes grew used to it, the cave appeared completely different from the night before.

They slowly turned in a circle.

"Look." Jennifer pointed.

The previous night, with the lantern at the bottom of the entrance and then hooked high in the cave's ceiling, the strong light had shown only the ramp beneath the entrance. With the diffuse light, they saw that the ramp was not fully across the entrance shaft but had a narrow depression in the wall beside it.

Jennifer turned on her flashlight. "It's another tunnel."

Mogi turned the lantern back on and they walked toward it.

It looked like a natural entrance that had been chiseled into a larger opening, with barely enough space to squeeze around a number of boulders jammed up against each other. Jennifer bent over and was slithering through the opening when she suddenly stopped. Backing up, she lowered her flashlight below the tops of the boulders and focused on the dirt in front of her.

It was a faint footprint—in the shape of a small shoe.

Looking ahead, she could see other footprints.

"Here goes," Jennifer said with a shaky voice. She took a deep breath and squiggled through the opening. It was a tight fit. She stepped up a series of boulders to the right, through a tilted slit between two rock slabs, and down into a larger opening. Mogi, having to bend sideways and contort his taller body to get through, used his hands to flounder onto the dirt before he could stand up. Once upright, he held the lantern as Jennifer carefully moved ahead.

It was another large room, almost the size of the entrance cave but with a slanted ceiling, making it feel much more cramped. Mogi sniffed. The air was moist, almost a misty-type moist. There must be water in here, he thought, moving forward a few feet.

A wall across from him lit up and sparkled in the lantern's light.

It took a few moments to understand. Reaching out his hand, he touched the surface of an almost vertical rock slab. Little streams of water parted around his fingers, joined again, and ran on down the rock surface. The wall shimmered like a wet, patterned shower curtain. Looking up, he could see a sheet of water seeping from a long crack across the top of the slab. It flowed down the rock face, gathering at the bottom in several small pools. Overflowing the pools, the water funneled through a jumble of rocks and disappeared.

Mogi pulled his fingers back, but the sparkle stayed on them. He moved his hand closer to the lantern. Tiny flakes of color clung to his fingertips.

Gold. Tiny flakes of gold.

The water must pass through a gold vein somewhere above, he thought. No telling for how long. Flowing over the rough surface of the rock for who knew how many years, the gold particles had coated it like scales on a fish.

Mogi slid his whole hand across the rock under the trickling waterfall. When he pulled it back, his hand wore a glove of gold.

He put his hand lightly back into the water and watched the dust wash off his hand, cascading down and swirling into small pools at the bottom of the wall. A shimmering bottom led him to kneel and put his finger through the clear surface of the largest pool.

There must be four inches of gold, he thought, as his finger wiggled through the loose metal flakes up to his palm, like a finger into sand.

"Wow."

This is where Crazy Bill got his gold dust.

As he focused on the wall, Jennifer was shining her flashlight around the chamber's ceiling and floor. It was certainly a natural formation, a cave created by large slabs of rock fallen together long ago, making tent-like sides to create the opening underneath. The floor was a heap of boulders and rocks.

Watching her feet, Jennifer moved carefully. She placed her hand on a rock to steady her steps and felt something under her fingers. She pulled back and turned her light to where her hand had been.

On top of the boulder was the stub of a candle, burnt until nothing remained except the wax drips on the sides of the rock. In the center, she could see the small remains of a wick.

She moved the flashlight to behind the boulder.

"Mogi," she called.

He moved to her side, moving the lantern to the far side of the boulder. They stood motionless for several moments. Moving around to a small rock close to the lantern, Jennifer carefully sat down. She took off her day-pack and unzipped it. She pulled out what to Mogi looked like a towel.

It was the baby blanket from Nancy's trunk.

Jennifer opened it up and laid it across the bones of the three children.

"They've been so cold for so long," she said with a sad and breaking voice as she tucked it lightly around the edges. Mogi set the lantern off to the side and wiped tears from his cheek.

The earth took our children
before our hearts were ready,
but our love remains.

CHAPTER
20

August 19, 1891

Jessie Jacobson saw the defiance in Maggie's eyes.

Jessie had told her at the start of the trail that she did not bring the key, that she was not going to open the trunk, and that they certainly were not going down into the shaft. They would just have to agree on a plan. She was resolute; that should have been enough.

But Maggie's eyes flared. She would not be denied.

Having to bring Matthew along didn't help one bit. He took Maggie's side and gave his sister no consideration at all. He hadn't been to the cabin, but he'd been thinking about it ever since he overheard the girls arguing about it. He didn't think he should be denied either.

Maggie went straight to prowling around the cabin, looking for something to use on the lock. Ignoring Jessie's lectures, she found a long-discarded iron skillet, swung it with deliberate force, and popped the first lock with hardly any effort. The second yielded just as easily.

Jessie realized it had all gone wrong and dissolved in tears of frustration.

Maggie stomped down on the trapdoor and brought it up. Balancing on the narrow lip inside the trunk, she stepped down the rungs of the ladder as if she deserved it.

Matthew was dazzled—the yawning hole so long hidden was like a birthday present. He pushed and shoved Jessie aside as he jumped over the trunk's side, grabbed the top rung, and stepped directly on Maggie's hand.

Jessie grabbed at her brother to yank him back up, mad at his insolence and mad at Maggie and mad at herself. She leaned over as she grabbed him—and slipped.

Suddenly, the trunk seemed to swallow the children, taking them in deeper with every frantic movement to save themselves.

As her foot slid, Jessie fell over the side of the trunk, her arms flailing at its sides and then at Matthew. He quickly ducked to miss her hands and stepped on Maggie's other hand as well. Maggie, jerking her hands away as she screamed in pain, pulled Matthew's feet off the ladder, leaving him hanging only by his hands. Jessie slid head first past Matthew onto Maggie as Matthew screamed and let go of the ladder.

Jessie's foot, swinging wildly, hit against the trunk lid, caught the trapdoor next to the hinge, and kicked the top of the ladder.

The trapdoor fell against the tangled, falling children and then slammed shut.

The trunk lid wobbled, slowly tipped over, and closed.

The ladder bent and broke, snapped from its hooks, and collapsed down the hole.

The three children fell in wriggling confusion to the top of an angled dirt ramp and slid into a rock chamber that was as dark as a moonless night.

For an instant, they were still. Then came the torrent of tears, shouts, and screams, until Maggie remembered her candles and matches. Once they were lighted, everyone felt better.

A month before, when Maggie had climbed down to the end of the ladder, she could not see past the entrance and did not feel the fear of the darkness. Now, with only the glow of three candles the children held, it seemed immense and never-ending, full of danger. Years of parental warnings about mines came back to the three children.

Immediately, they struggled to climb up to the trapdoor, but the wooden part of the shaft had nothing to grab on to and nothing to step on.

They tried to get the ladder back up to the entrance, but it was long and ungainly, and one leg had broken. Even partially propped up, stepping on a rung made it swivel, turn, and slide out of the hole time and again. They kicked the metal hooks out of the way, unaware of their function.

They couldn't make anything work.

The three searched for another way out, coming to the long tunnel and going down it. When they got to the opening behind the waterfall, they understood immediately what it was. All three tried to get to the opening, to look down, to see their parents and the others, to yell as loudly as they could, to throw rocks to get their attention, to do anything to call for help. But the frenzy of spray bouncing off the rock walls, the tunnel ceiling dripping with water, the puddles on the floor shaking with a booming and thundering that hurt their ears kept them from getting close. Knowing that all those people were just below them and yet so untouchable threw them into sobs and screams. Fearing that Maggie or Matthew might panic and rush into the massive column of water and be pounded to death on the rocks below, Jessie grabbed them by the arms and dragged them back up the tunnel, all of them quivering in the darkness from the cold of their sodden clothes.

The children found the room with the glittering wall. It at least felt smaller and more cheery, so that's where they stayed. Maggie had dropped her candle in the other tunnel, so Matthew's was set on a rock. Holding their hands close to the flame for warmth, they found nothing to say.

Jessie tried again. Using the last candle, she went back to the first chamber and struggled on her own with the ladder. She found it impossible and soon dissolved in tears.

She was scared, she was sad, and she was alone. She was responsible for the others but could find no means of rescue.

She had set her candle on the ground as she worked with the ladder, and then knocked it over. The flame went out. Flailing about the floor for several minutes, she knew it was lost. It was only by the tiniest light from the slit in the rocks that she found her way back to the others.

They held each other for warmth and watched as the candle burned, flickered, and then glowed with only an ember.

Then it was dark again.

And it was very cold.

CHAPTER

The Present

Nudging aside the blanket when they had to, Mogi and Jennifer carefully, reverently, inspected the floor behind the rocks. Scraps of delicate lace and cloth from the dresses were draped in a heap and the buckles were dull in the lantern light. The shoes were complete, the leather bent and shrunken. Long strands of hair were mixed with the dirt of the floor, matted from the moisture in the air.

Jennifer touched lightly, not moving or disturbing the bones. She leaned forward, close to the girl she knew was Jessie. She carefully, so carefully, felt around the bottom of the skull. When her fingers touched a cold piece of metal, she took it into her hand. Looking at it closely by the lantern light, she put it into her pocket, replaced the blanket, stood, and turned to Mogi.

"I'm ready to go," she said quietly.

Mogi had decided not to take pictures. It would have been disrespectful, like sitting on somebody's grave.

They stepped around the rocks, back to the golden wall.

"Crazy Bill must have found this and knew he had to protect it against anybody and everybody," Mogi said.

"That's why he worked so hard at hiding the entrance. He probably imagined the whole mountain was gold. And from the other tunnel we found, he was probably going to dig out of the main chamber, up, and back around so he'd end up above this room. He knew he'd hit the gold vein somewhere. Meanwhile, he could live off the gold flakes at the bottom of the wall."

Finding it hard to not look back, they squeezed through the boulders into the original chamber and back up through the trunk. Mogi closed the trapdoor and replaced the bark and needles to conceal it.

They turned off the lantern and sat on the porch with their backs against the cabin wall. The barest sliver of color from the sunset was on the bottom of the clouds. The canyon was dark.

"What do you think they'll do with this?" Mogi asked his sister.

"I'm not sure, but they'll do something," Jennifer responded. "If it were just an answer to a couple of legends, they might take pictures and make an exhibit at the museum. But the gold changes everything. They'll have to remove the gold or people will continually try to get at it. Maybe it'll even become a real mine. You know that somebody will make the argument that the town needs the money. I don't know."

A curtain of mist and light rain settled over the forest, turning off the final glow of evening.

The siblings were content to sit outside the cabin and draw in the sweet, moist air of the Rockies. They had found the lost children. Jennifer had found Jessie.

* * *

Climbing back up to the Jeep was too dangerous in the dark, not to mention the foolishness of driving the trail at night.

"Jimmy and I will come back tomorrow and get it," Mogi said as he worked his way down the trail by flashlight.

"Hold it," he said suddenly, moving quickly into a crouch. Mogi turned off his light and slid off the trail with Jennifer, hunkering behind a bush.

There were two black Suburbans pulled over to the edge of the parking lot, both with their rear doors open. Floodlights on the roofs lit the ground in front and behind. One man was packing away a transit while another picked through a number of boxes on the asphalt, then lifted each onto the tailgate. In the glare of the lights, several small flags were visible stuck into the earth across the picnic grounds.

"Those flags mean they've been laying out survey lines. Condominiums, I betcha," Mogi whispered to Jennifer.

"That's not right; it has to be something else," she said. "Nancy told me the CEO specifically mentioned that he was going to preserve the land as a public park."

"Hmmm . . . ." Mogi said. "It doesn't look like they're planning on preserving anything. Typical work would have shut down while it was still light, so these guys must be rushing to get something finished."

Piling in all the boxes and closing the tailgates, the men got in, and the Suburbans pulled out and down the road.

Mogi and Jennifer stood up and cautiously moved to the area with tables. Making a circuit around the edges and up toward Thunder Falls, they found several wooden stakes scattered among the flags. Numbers were written on the side.

"Probably elevation differences," Mogi said.

Jennifer sighed. "Maybe you're right. Homes for the rich and famous."

"That's why they blocked the road. It wasn't about us at all. Mudslide, my foot!" Mogi said in an angry voice. "The Millennium Corporation isn't waiting for any town vote to get started. They think they've got it whipped.

"Homes in this canyon, with these views and a waterfall in the backyard, would sell like hotcakes."

Mogi reached for his phone. He would call Jimmy and Nancy, tell them what they'd found, and beg for a ride home.

Jennifer stopped his hand. "I think I need the walk. We'll be back soon enough. I'm not quite ready to get back into Nancy's war."

Setting an easy pace, the two walked the center of the pavement as they watched the town lights brighten and the sky darken. When they reached the landslide of dirt across the road, they could see where tire tracks had crossed over the lower end and then been covered over by a backhoe, standing silent on the other side.

Skirting the dirt, they silently enjoyed the walk. The two siblings went to the apartment, got Jennifer's car, and drove to Nancy's. The lights were on, and her car was out front. In the living room, they passed several stacks of bundled newspapers on the floor that smelled of fresh printing.

Jimmy was slumped at the table, his head leaning back, while Nancy leaned forward, her chin resting on her crossed arms. Only her eyes moved as the two came in. Any attempt at saying hello was met with mutters. Mogi and Jennifer sagged into the empty chairs at the table.

Nancy's eyes were bloodshot and tired. It looked as if she had something to say but couldn't focus her thoughts to form the words.

Jennifer drew her chair around the table, closer to Nancy's side. She reached into her pocket, looked into her friend's eyes, opened her hand, and slowly lowered the locket into Nancy's palm.

It was a small, pretty locket in the shape of a heart, identical to the one cast in bronze hanging around the neck of the tall girl in a statue across town.

The kind of locket a mother gives her daughter.

Jennifer wrapped Nancy's fingers around it as Nancy's eyes widened with recognition. Her eyes filling with tears, Nancy lowered her head to the table and cried, not quietly but with heaving shoulders, tears coming from hurt and weariness and an exhausted heart.

*　　*　　*

Mogi and Jennifer described their perilous trip across the mountains and their discoveries beneath the cabin.

"I wondered where my Jeep was," Jimmy said. "I figured you two were taking good care of it. Sounds like you did. That Jeep road is pretty cool, huh?"

Jennifer looked at him with meekness in her eyes. "Well, at one point, I believe I peed in your seat."

Nancy sat back with a little smile, looking relieved at having finally cried.

"I've never been so angry. I'm really embarrassed. I hope you can forgive me," Nancy confided. "A fool is what I've been. And a childish fool, at that. It was the faces of the people in Montrose that made me realize what I was doing. The editor kept shaking his head as he read the text on the screen. It was plain that he didn't want to have anything to do with my words. He went ahead, though, and the printers got the papers assembled and loaded up, but I saw doom in their eyes, just like his.

"Anyway, that's all it took. I guess I can use all of this for starting fires in the winter," she said as she swept her hand toward the bundles. "And I'm embarrassed for myself. You've solved a hundred-year old mystery, you've made the real difference to the town, and I've done nothing but increase the hurt."

"What are you going to do now?" Jennifer asked.

Nancy shrugged and shook her head with an expression of resignation. "I don't know. I think I've lost."

Jennifer looked around the room at the other tired faces, then back to Nancy.

"If you don't mind me making a suggestion," she said, "I have an idea."

CHAPTER
22

Mogi and Jennifer called their parents early the next day for permission to stay longer, spending almost an hour telling of the week's adventures and discoveries. Mogi texted pictures of the statue, the waterfall, and the cabin, and sent them the web addresses for more of the story of the lost children.

While they were busy on the phone, Jimmy contacted a couple of the men who worked at the Hummingbird Mine north of Ouray, explained the situation, and received an immediate offer to bring a generator, lights, and a new ladder to the cabin and get everything set up so people could go into the mine.

By mid-morning, a caravan of cars and pickups wound its way up Thunder Canyon. A county bulldozer scraped back the "mudslide" to let them through.

A generator was soon noisily providing the power for several strands of lights running along the floor of the caves and tunnels. A new ladder replaced Crazy Bill's. After a special team from the Hummingbird removed the box of dynamite, Mogi, Jennifer, Nancy, and Jimmy led the first explorers into Crazy Bill's mine.

Nancy was very pleased when the mayor could not, by

any position whatsoever, fit his body through the slit into the gold room where the children rested. He fumed as he waited in the big chamber.

Photographers took over from there, taking hundreds of pictures of the cave, the equipment, and the bones. The people, the noise, and the activity overwhelmed the privacy of the night before, so Jennifer took her brother's hand and led him outside to the far end of the porch where they sat and talked.

The next day, a special edition of the Ouray newspaper was delivered across town. It was dedicated to three children who lived in Ouray in 1891 and who had vanished during a picnic. Featuring several pictures of the mine, the skeletons, the cabin, the trunk, and the statue, the special edition was a tribute to the people of Ouray, both past and present.

The main article was a personal story by Nancy. It spoke of growing up in a small town surrounded by heaven. It was a gift, she said. She told of hearing, believing, and living the stories handed down by the successive generations of mountain people.

Jennifer especially liked the opening paragraph:

> I've always thought of Ouray in terms of hard granite, tough people, and harsh winters. What I find as I grow older is a preciousness and fragility to what we have. Life could be easier in other towns, yet we stay. And we stay willingly because Ouray is a part of us and we are a part of it. Leaving or drastically changing it would be like selling our birthright. My birthright is a

gift from the generations before me. It is a
description of who I am, of who I want to
be, of what I care about, of what I believe
is worth living for. Living my birthright is
my gift to those who come after me.

All of the copies disappeared in less than an hour.
Nancy, with a smile of pride, promised that more would
soon be printed.

She need not have been concerned. The newspaper
publisher in Montrose was already printing a thousand
more while sending the story over the web.

It took only a day for the story to go viral.

The skeletons of the children were carefully removed
and taken to the hospital. There was talk about recon-
struction, exhibits and glass cases, and a hundred other
ways of displaying the bones.

In the end, there was a simple funeral. In a special casket
brought from Denver, the three children were buried together, the tall girl cradling a worn doll in her arms and
wearing a heart-shaped locket around her neck, the three
children quietly nestled under an old baby blanket.

*   *   *

The Colorado Highway Patrol escorted the funeral
procession from the church to the cemetery. It took almost an hour to travel the five miles. Every road, every
street, every empty lot overflowed with vehicles.

The townspeople had planned a simple memorial service
at the Foursquare Church close to downtown. But as soon
as the sun shone on the distant peaks, every sort of vehicle

imaginable—cars, buses, vans, motor homes, four-wheel drives, motorcycles—surged into the streets of Ouray. The town leaders, faced with the impossibility of accommodating everyone, decided to move the ceremony to the cemetery.

Placing a few quick phone calls, the mayor asked that all the pastures next to the cemetery be opened for parking. By the time the word was spread and traffic sent in the right direction, the scheduled service time had come and gone.

The vehicles kept arriving, and people kept pouring in. With the highway patrol nudging through the crowd with great difficulty, the hearse finally pulled up to the gravesite. So that no one was excluded, the ceremony was delayed. The Foursquare Gospel choir performed well, though it had to sing almost every song in its songbooks to fill in the time.

The four friends rode in the funeral procession as representatives of the family. As they left the car and came to the grave, they could see that the iron fence had been dismantled and set to the side, along with the angels. The grass had been cut and a large hole readied.

"This is incredible," Mogi whispered to Jennifer. "There must be thousands of people." It seemed like an endless stream of people crowding into the cemetery.

Nancy leaned closer and nodded toward the highway. A black Chevy Suburban muscled its way to the cemetery gate and let out its passengers. Three men joined the fringes of the crowd and began working their way to the front.

"The guy in the gray suit is Mister Big, Henry David Williams. The other two guys must be henchmen. I don't see Mister Jerk. He was probably too busy designing condominiums to come."

Finally under way, the service was simple, direct, and without pretension. The minister, having spoken a few words while alternating with the choir and hymns sung by the whole gathering, motioned to Nancy. She stepped next to him, adjusted the microphone, took a page of notes from her pocket, and addressed the crowd in a clear voice.

"I've always thought of Ouray in terms of hard granite, tough people, and harsh winters," she began. "What I have found as I grow older is a preciousness and fragility to what we have."

It was her article from the special edition, specially requested by the mayor and the town council. But she had no need to read from the page. Instead, she looked at the crowd as she spoke the words. She spoke from her heart, watching the sea of faces as their eyes softened and their heads nodded.

They had come from all over. Not only the nearby towns of Durango, Silverton, and Telluride but also from Leadville, Frisco, Denver, Colorado Springs, and dozens of other Colorado towns—wherever there was a history of mining, a history of the frontier, a history of people who made do with what they had, a history of people who endured. They came from places where people felt a birthright to a country that had taken them in and given them homes and lives.

They came because of three children. Three children who were lost and had been found. Three children who had come, in a few short days, to represent the cost of that birthright. The cost of any birthright.

Henry David Williams, his eyes sometimes moving across the faces in the crowd, watched in wonder. Jennifer could see that in his hand he held a copy of the special edition.

During the last prayer, not a sound could be heard except the calm, steady voice of the minister. After the amen, the crowd relaxed, but the people continued to stand together. They didn't want to leave. Something held them; something bound them to the preciousness of the moment.

After a few minutes, the bond loosened and people moved toward the road, the pasture, the town.

A line formed next to the gravesite, and a mound of flowers soon grew next to it, people saying goodbye to three children they had not known. The four friends circled about each other and enjoyed the quiet pressure of a common hug.

Nancy felt a hand on her shoulder. She turned around.

"May I speak with you privately?" Henry David Williams asked in a soft voice.

Nancy agreed, and the two walked down the line of gravestones until they approached a granite bench and sat.

"I liked your article. I liked it a lot," he said. "I believe that you and your friends have done something extremely special, something that this town, and this country, will not stop feeling for a long time."

He smiled.

"And it's a feeling that's far beyond anything I could ever afford and could ever hope to imitate. I believe the corporation will have to build the world's greatest resort town someplace else. And while all those rich people will be there, I'll come here."

Nancy's mouth fell open.

"But I must sincerely apologize for the behavior of Mr. Harrison," he continued. "I told you once that my family had a history with the Pennsylvania coal mines. To be honest, I grew up in a small coal town. My father was a miner, as was his father. We were poor, and I remember how much I hated the coal company for forcing us into what felt like slavery. They were probably not as bad as all that, but the company certainly cared more about profits than the quality of the miners' lives.

"When I discovered that Montgomery Harrison was bullying anyone who stood in his way, I was reminded of how my parents must have felt. I'm ashamed that I was unaware of his actions, and I apologize. Mr. Harrison is no longer with the company."

Nancy closed her mouth and gave a little smile. She had a fleeting vision of Montgomery Harrison working behind the counter at McDonald's.

"But I want to say more," Williams continued. "I spoke of the importance to me of Ouray's values during our first meeting, and I'll speak of them again now. Your article reminded me of who I am, what I wanted to be, and what I should be doing with my wealth. I would like to advise you that, though buying the town is no longer an objective, I think I can provide some good to the people who live here.

"So, I'm keeping the hotel at the end of town. It'll be fun to fix up, but increasing the number of bathrooms there will require a better city sewer system, which I will help the town build. I also expect my guests to have reliable internet and phone service, so I'll be negotiating with the local communications company to upgrade all the equipment in the town and provide wireless for every business."

Nancy's mouth had opened again in disbelief. "You would do all this for us?" she asked.

Williams looked thoughtful. "I'm not doing it for you. I'm doing it for me. And my children. It's been a long time since I've thought of myself having a birthright. If I have one, then I need to reclaim it, so I can also pass it on to my family. I can tell you this: Passing on a birthright will be a whole lot more satisfying than just leaving a pile of money."

He said a few more words, apologized for needing to run to another meeting, shook Nancy's hand warmly, and was picked up at the cemetery gate by the Suburban.

Nancy was still stunned as she returned to her friends and told them what he had said. Then reporters quickly pulled her away for interviews and statements.

As the crowd drifted back to their vehicles, Mogi and Jennifer walked around the cemetery, much as they had done just a few days before—reading the gravestones, looking at the worn carvings, wondering about the people buried there.

"That was a nice thing for him to do, offering to rebuild the hotel and everything else," Mogi said as they strolled along.

"It was. It'll take care of some of the big problems that Nancy talked about, which should help the town address some of its other needs. Maybe even the mayor will stop being a butthead and help instead of getting in the way."

"You think Nancy will get her job back?"

"Oh, yeah. People will be falling all over themselves trying to apologize for getting carried away by dollar signs. She'll love it too. She might dream of New York, but she's a mountain girl. Even if Henry David Williams had decided not to stick with the hotel, things will be getting better, and she'll be right in the middle of it. His generosity will be appreciated—new money is always good—but the people who live here are survivors just like Nancy. I don't know what they're going to do with the mine or the gold, but the town has a new story now, about lost children being found and a fabulous gold mine that people have been walking on top of all these years without knowing about it. A really good story can give all sorts of new life to a little town. The people here will be happier than ever, without having to give up any of their history."

"You know," Mogi said, stopping in front of a large headstone, "I was trying to figure out how so many extraordinary people ended up in one place. Now I think that they weren't extraordinary at all. I bet almost everybody was plain, everyday ordinary. Common men and women who came here to find new work, new lives, new adventures, maybe new beginnings. They were just ordinary people who ended up doing extraordinary things."

The next week, the statue of *The Lost Children* was moved from the museum's side garden and placed inside the old wrought-iron fence at the head of the grave. There it would remain, the three angels now gathered at its base, the last official statement that three children had lived and that someone had loved them.

CHAPTER

The air was extremely dry, the sun extremely hot, the land extremely big, and the scenery so bare of vegetation that it looked like the moon.

Mogi smiled. The country of the San Juan River was appearing on the horizon, and it was good to be home.

Jennifer drove with a quiet heart, thinking about all that had happened. The mayor and town council were having a wonderful time arguing about what to do with their new gold mine, businesses in town were booming, and the bar at the Big Corral Steakhouse was even offering a Mogi & Jen mixed drink, with free peanuts.

Mom's really going to love that, she thought.

Not talking much, still weary from the thousands of questions during the days before, Jennifer was content to float with the scenery. Content and comfortable.

But it didn't last long.

"Wait a minute," Jennifer suddenly said. "What about the ghost of Crazy Bill's cabin? You never figured out what happened with that."

Mogi looked at her and smiled.

"Ah, the ghost. I forgot to tell you. Remember the guys that Jimmy knew? From the Hummingbird mine?

After they went through the chambers and tunnels, I sat down and talked with them. When I mentioned the original Crazy Bill story, they thought it was obvious what happened.

"Any time you dig into a solid rock mountain, you let out trapped gas, gas that normally contains bad stuff like cyanide. When Crazy Bill was working in the mine and the trapdoor was open, it wasn't dangerous. But when the air pressure was low outside, like during a storm, and the trapdoor hadn't been opened for while, like when he might have been gone somewhere, the gas would seep out of the rock and collect in the chamber. Opening the trapdoor would let the stored-up gas escape into the cabin. If Ol' Bill didn't have the door open, he literally flooded his cabin with poisonous vapors. Sometimes cyanide gas has an odor, but sometimes it doesn't. I guess this time, it didn't.

"He must have been in the cabin when gas came up from the mine. Cyanide makes your muscles contract, your arms and legs twist and stiffen. The muscles of your face tighten up, making your eyes bulge, your lips pull back, and your tongue swell. Your blood vessels pop.

"It must be an awful sight. If someone didn't know better, your face could look like you'd been scared to death. It must have been a horrible way to die."

Jennifer grew pale.

"Is that what happened to the children?" she asked.

Mogi touched her hand.

"I asked. They didn't think so. It had been years since any new rock had been broken, so no gas was probably in the mine. The children were together when we found them, probably huddled together for warmth. I expect they died very quietly from the cold. It would not have hurt in the end. They would have just gone to sleep."

Jennifer drove without asking more, and Mogi let her have the quiet space.

He was thinking about what to do with his new prize possessions—a photograph, an old iron key, and the rubbing from the plaque at the gravesite.

The picture showed the statue of the three children next to the museum. Jennifer was reaching up in the picture to the face of the tall child, caressing her cheek as if comforting her, telling her that she would never be lost again. The photo reminded him of how much his sister put up with his craziness but still continued to love him.

The old key was an antique, the kind made with a hollow shaft.

And the rubbing? He thought he might put it in a frame and hang it on his wall.

Jennifer was right. When he touched the rubbing, felt its roughness and read the words, it was something more than information. He felt the texture of people's lives, of the struggles and victories, the sorrows and joys.

As she drove, Jennifer too was working on a plan for the evening. She needed to rearrange her room for a new piece of furniture—an old camelback trunk.

Not very big, with wood and tin around the sides, and a tin top stamped with tiny stars.

COMING IN SEPTEMBER 2017
Book 3 of the Mogi Franklin Mysteries: The Secret of La Rosa

Mogi Franklin, his sister Jennifer, and their cousin Jeremy start into the snow-covered mountains of New Mexico for a cross-country ski trip. But a vicious blizzard blinds their way, and they barely survive to wake up in a mysterious Spanish hacienda. Within a day, they find themselves the prime suspects in the theft of a religious icon—an icon that is key to solving an ancient legend of missing Spanish gold.

ABOUT THE AUTHOR

Don Willerton was raised in a small oil boomtown in the Panhandle of Texas, becoming familiar through family vacations with the northern New Mexico area where he now makes his home.

After earning a degree in physics from Midwestern State University in Texas and a master's in computer science and electrical engineering from the University of New Mexico, he worked for Los Alamos National Laboratory for almost three decades.

During his career there, Willerton was a supercomputer programmer for a number of years and a manager after that for "way too long," and also worked on information policy and cyber-security.

He finds focusing on only one thing very difficult among such varied interests as home building, climbing Colorado's tallest peaks, and rafting the rivers of the Southwest (including the Colorado through Grand Canyon). Willerton also has owned a handyman business for a number of years, rebuilt old cars, and made furniture in his woodshop.

He is a wanderer in both mind and body, fascinated with history and its landscape, varied peoples and their cultures, good mysteries, secrets, and seeking out treasure. Most of all, he loves the outdoors and the places he finds in the Southwest where spirits live and ghosts dance. Weaving it all together to share with readers has been the driving force of Willerton's writing over the past twenty years.

The Lost Children is the second novel in the nine-book Mogi Franklin series of Southwest-based mysteries for middle-grade boys and girls.